Praise for *Killer Swell*,
the first Noah Braddock mystery

"Sharp dialogue and splashy local color make Shelby's first outing more fun than a day at the beach."

—*Kirkus Reviews*

"Jeff Shelby grew up in and around the Southern California surfing fraternity; he knows the territory and puts his knowledge to good use. He writes crisply, cleanly and—praise be!—economically, a virtue seldom found in first novels."

—*The San Diego Union-Tribune*

"Snappy dialogue and descriptions give the book a bad-boy edge."

—*The Washington Post*

"Shelby writes like a pro, with realistic characters, terrific plotting, and a setting that makes you want to jump into your Jams and wax up your board."

—*The Kansas City Star*

"A heck of a detective, whose surfer appearance belies a thoughtful, tough, hardworking guy who knows his way around an investigation. . . . Shelby has written a serious detective story with a generous helping of humor."

—*Detroit Free Press*

ued . . .

"Crisp and engaging." —*San Diego Magazine*

"An impressive first effort. Braddock lives by his own code, like so many fictional private eyes. But he's surrounded by a strong supporting cast, particularly Liz Santangelo, a detective with the San Diego police and Braddock's ex-girlfriend. This promises to be a series worth following." —*The Albany Times Union*

"While the mystery contains surprising twists and turns, the real joy in this book is the characters."
—*The Denver Post*

"California backdrops, an engaging, in-your-face, surfer-versus-the-establishment attitude, and former relationship complications make this a strongly recommended new series start."
—*Library Journal* (starred review)

Wicked Break

A NOAH BRADDOCK NOVEL

JEFF SHELBY

AN ONYX BOOK

ONYX
Published by New American Library, a division of
Penguin Group (USA) Inc., 375 Hudson Street,
New York, New York 10014, USA
Penguin Group (Canada), 90 Eglinton Avenue East, Suite 700, Toronto,
Ontario M4P 2Y3, Canada (a division of Pearson Penguin Canada Inc.)
Penguin Books Ltd., 80 Strand, London WC2R 0RL, England
Penguin Ireland, 25 St. Stephen's Green, Dublin 2,
Ireland (a division of Penguin Books Ltd.)
Penguin Group (Australia), 250 Camberwell Road, Camberwell, Victoria 3124,
Australia (a division of Pearson Australia Group Pty. Ltd.)
Penguin Books India Pvt. Ltd., 11 Community Centre, Panchsheel Park,
New Delhi - 110 017, India
Penguin Group (NZ), 67 Apollo Drive, Rosedale, North Shore,
Auckland 1311, New Zealand (a division of Pearson New Zealand Ltd.)
Penguin Books (South Africa) (Pty.) Ltd., 24 Sturdee Avenue,
Rosebank, Johannesburg 2196, South Africa

Penguin Books Ltd., Registered Offices:
80 Strand, London WC2R 0RL, England

Published by Onyx, an imprint of New American Library, a division of Penguin Group (USA) Inc. Previously published in a Dutton edition.

First Onyx Printing, June 2007
10 9 8 7 6 5 4 3 2 1

For Stephanie

1

The man on the shore was waiting for me.

I'd been in the water for an hour, catching a nice southern break that was producing tight swells of about three to four feet just north of the jetty in Mission Beach. He'd been there for about half that time, watching from a distance, and when I dug the nose of my six-foot Ron Jon into the face of an anxiety-free wave and went ass-over-kettle into the water, the distraction of being watched ended my session.

I trudged in, shaking the ocean out of my hair as I approached the shoreline. The beach was deserted on a cloudy Monday at midmorning. When the man waved at me, I knew he wasn't trying to get anyone's attention but mine.

"Are you Noah?" he asked. "Noah Braddock?"

I ran a hand over my face, sliding away the excess water and not bothering to disguise a frown. I jammed the butt of the board into the sand and let it stand erect. "Yeah. Who are you?"

"I'm Peter Pluto," he said. "I need your help. I need you to find my brother." He gestured behind him. "The guy at your place said you were out here. Your roommate, I assumed."

Carter was not my roommate, but inhabited my place nearly as much as I did.

I studied Peter Pluto. He wore blue jeans and a brown sweatshirt with old running shoes. His thinning dark hair was trimmed short and the lines in his face told me he hadn't slept much recently.

I bent down and undid the Velcro leash around my right ankle. "That right?"

"You are an investigator, aren't you?" he asked, squatting down a little, trying to get even with my face.

I stood back up. "Yeah, I am. But I'm not doing a whole lot of work right now."

"I'll make it worth your while," Peter Pluto said. "Cash up front."

"It's not about the money, Mr. Pluto," I said. "I'm just not looking for work at the moment. Other things going on, you know?"

"Peter. Call me Peter." He blinked a couple of times and, for a moment, I thought he might cry. But he shifted his eyes and sighed. "I guess Mr. Berkley was wrong."

I looked at him, surprised. "You know Berk?"

Pluto nodded. "Yeah. He handled my mother's estate when she died. That's how I got your name. Said you'd be able to help me."

Mike Berkley was an attorney who had thrown me some work when I first started out as an investigator. I was having a hard time paying the bills and he'd come through with some simple stuff that had kept me out of complete poverty. Berk had become a friend and I didn't think he would've offered my name without reason.

"Tell me about your brother," I said, pulling my rash guard up over my head.

Pluto looked at me cautiously for a moment, perhaps wondering if I was serious. He relaxed when he saw that I was.

"His name is Linc and he's nineteen," Pluto said. "He's been gone for at least a couple of days."

"Have you gone to the police?"

He hesitated, something crossing his eyes that I couldn't read.

"I don't think the police will do anything," he said. "He's legal and he's run away before."

"Run away?"

Pluto nodded. "About four years ago. Before our mom passed away. She had cancer and it was tough on him."

"Where were you?"

He shifted uncomfortably, kicking his right shoe into the sand. "Basically, I'd left him there. It was tough on me, too. I was going to school up at UCLA. I didn't make it home very often, I guess."

I nodded. "So where is he living now?"

"Up in the college area," he said, referring to the neighborhoods around San Diego State. "When Mom died two years ago, he was emancipated and has lived on his own since."

"How come not with you? Or your father?"

A small wave of anger spread across his face. "We didn't really have a dad."

I knew the feeling. I didn't push it.

"As for why Linc didn't live with me—well, he hates me." Peter Pluto gave a half-smile, sadness and shame creeping into his eyes. "Blames me for not sticking around and for leaving him with her. When she died, I tried to get him to come live with me. But he wouldn't do it. There was a small trust from our grandparents. He's managed to make it last for a while. Won't take my help."

"But now you want to help."

He nodded. "I check up on him once a week. Knock on his door, he tells me to fuck off. At least I know he's alright. I went there Friday and no one answered. Tried Saturday and yesterday. Nothing."

"How do you know he didn't just take off for a few days?" I asked. "A little vacation or something."

Pluto shook his head sternly. "That's not him. He's going to State, majoring in political science. Wants to be an attorney, I guess. Plus, it's almost midterm time."

"Midterms usually . . . mean bigger parties at State," I said, scoffing at the notion that anyone took exams seriously up on Montezuma Mesa.

Pluto shook his head.

"Maybe he just needed to blow off a little steam," I said. "Get away for a day or two."

"He doesn't do that kind of thing. He's serious about school."

I thought Peter was kidding himself. San Diego State is the bastard child of San Diego universities. It lacks the private prestige and pricey tuition of USD and doesn't come close to the scientific reputation of UCSD. The students who ended up there did so because they were denied admission to the other two schools or simply because they didn't want their studies to get in the way of partying.

As an undistinguished alum, I knew that from experience.

"Your best bet is still to report it to the police," I said. "Even if he's run away before, you can file a missing persons report. I can give you the name of someone who will listen to you and take you seriously."

Whatever had crossed his eyes before when I'd mentioned the police was back.

"I can't go to the police," he said.

"Why not?"

He took a deep breath and shoved his hands into the pockets of his jeans. "I went into his apartment, okay? I talked the super into letting me in yesterday because I was worried." He stopped, his face tightening. "And I found something."

I didn't say anything.

"There were guns in his dresser," Peter Pluto finally said. "A ton of them. I don't know anything about guns, but there were some that looked like handguns and some that looked like things I've seen in movies. Automatics, maybe, like machine guns. I freaked out and left."

I flicked a bead of water off my arm. Peter wasn't doing much to convince me to find his brother. "So he's not totally serious about school, I guess."

He yanked his hands out of his pockets, his face coloring. "He must have gotten hooked up with a bad crowd. Look, he's had a tough time with everything that's happened." The color receded from his face and a look of utter frustration and concern replaced it. "If he needs help, I want to help him. But I don't want him to go to jail." He stared at me with desperate eyes. "Mike said you could help. Can you?"

I gazed at Peter Pluto for a moment. The last time I'd gotten involved in a family affair, I'd been shot at, Carter had nearly died, and I'd pushed a woman to her death. I didn't want to wade into that kind of mess again.

But I'd lied about not needing work. Truth was, I hadn't seen any good money in a while. A new Jeep payment and a surf trip to Cabo had eaten quickly through my small savings account. I was going to need to do something soon.

Maybe this wouldn't be so personal, though. Do the work, find the kid, get paid. I didn't know Peter or his brother. I figured my past would have a tough time getting in the middle of this one.

And there was something about standing on a quiet beach under thick gray clouds with a man who clearly cared about his brother that made me vulnerable.

"Give me the address," I said to Peter Pluto.

2

I asked Peter a few more questions about the guns he'd seen because I wanted a better idea of what I might be getting myself into. But he clearly knew nothing about guns and the tension on his face told me that finding them had really shocked the hell out of him. I knew I'd have to go look for myself. He gave me a wallet-sized photo of Linc and I told him I'd be in touch after I checked out the apartment.

I went back to my place, dropping my board on the patio that faced the beach. Carter had apparently anticipated my irritation with him and vacated the premises. Not as dumb as he looked.

I showered and changed into a pair of corduroy board shorts and a T-shirt. I grabbed an apple and a soda from the fridge and headed out to see where Linc Pluto lived.

I pointed my Jeep east, going past the Bahia and the bay, getting onto Interstate 8 behind the old Sports

Arena. The freeway cut through Mission Valley, bisecting the giant canyon that now housed a golf course, several shopping centers, and Qualcomm Stadium. Just before I hit La Mesa, I took the College Avenue exit and headed south.

The area around San Diego State was trying to reinvent itself, just like other older parts of the city. The university wanted to sell itself as a destination school rather than a state school and they were hoping to create a college-town feel. Abandoned strip malls had been rebuilt with fast-food joints and cafés. But the new neon of the signs in the windows hadn't deterred those who had been used to the old ways of the neighborhood. You were safe during the day, but you didn't venture out at night unless you were with your frat pals.

I hung a left on El Cajon Boulevard and found Linc's address just past the old Campus Drive-in. His apartment was in an ugly L-shaped two-story building, with an old asphalt lot in front. The stucco exterior was painted drab brown and the doors were a shade darker. Could've been an old motel.

I parked in the lot and found Linc's door on the ground level. A small window sat just to the right of the door.

I knocked, but got no answer.

I tried the door, but it didn't open.

I looked in the window, but saw no one.

Nowhere fast.

I walked down to the next door. Bob Marley crooned softly behind it.

I knocked.

Footsteps came closer and the door swung open.

A girl of about twenty or so stood in front of me. A tight olive tank top hugged the curves of her chest, cutoff cargo shorts exposed long tan legs. Her hair was a mess of dirty brown dreadlocks piled on top of her head. The thin silver hoops in her earlobes matched the ones in her eyebrow and bottom lip. She was attractive in an I'm-in-college-and-rebelling kind of way.

Her emerald eyes flashed and she looked annoyed. "What?"

"I'm looking for your neighbor."

"Did you try his place?"

I smiled. "Yeah. He's not there. Any idea where I could find him?"

She folded her arms across her chest. "Who are you?"

"Noah Braddock. I'm an investigator. Who are you?"

"Dana Madison." She looked at me with new interest. "An investigator. No shit?"

"None whatsoever."

"And you're looking for Linc?"

"I am."

"Well, I don't know where he is," she said. "But Rachel might."

"Rachel?"

"My roommate." She looked me up and down with a confidence she couldn't possibly have been old enough to possess. A slow smile emerged on her face and she stepped to the side. "Right this way, stud."

I felt dirty, but in a good way, and stepped past her into the apartment.

Dana went and turned down the stereo in the corner. The interior was sparsely furnished and the white paint on the walls was cracking. The aroma of freshly smoked marijuana filled the room. A small television sat on a banged-up hutch. A worn wooden coffee table stood in the middle of the room just across from a tattered brown sofa. A Donald Duck bong grinned at me from the tabletop.

First Pluto, now Donald.

Disney appeared to be overtaking my life.

"You see where the spout is on him?" Dana said, coming over to the sofa and noticing I was looking at Donald.

"Uh, yeah."

"Makes it look like you're giving him a hummer when you spark up."

"Cool."

"I know," she said, missing my sarcasm.

"So. Rachel?"

Dana nodded, still looking at me. "You have to be in such a hurry?"

"Busy, busy."

A smile curled onto her lips. "I'd like to see you get busy." She turned toward the hallway that extended off the room and yelled, "Rachel. Somebody here for you."

A scuffling sound came from down the hallway, followed by footsteps. Rachel emerged.

If Dana was attractive, Rachel was a flat-out knock-out. A fiery mane of red hair cascaded around her tan, oval face. She wore jean shorts frayed at the ends and a tight black top, exposing a drum-tight abdomen and a tiny diamond in her navel. Her arms and legs were as tan as her face, toned like her stomach. The only imperfection I could see was that her large brown eyes were ringed with bright red blood vessels.

She looked at me, confused. "Hi."

"Hi."

"This is Noah," Dana said. "He's a private investigator."

Rachel gave me a blank stare. "Oh."

"I'm looking for Linc," I said. "Next door."

"Oh."

"You know him?"

"Yeah, she does," Dana said, then giggled.

Rachel looked at her. "Yeah, I do." Then she giggled.

Stoners can be frustrating.

I took a deep breath. "How do you know him?"

Rachel folded her arms across her chest. "From school."

"And you guys are friends?"

"Yeah, they are," Dana said, and snickered again.

"Shut up," Rachel said to her, then burst into giggles again as well. She composed herself quickly. "We're friends."

"Friends?"

Rachel blinked several times. "He tutored me."

Dana laughed out loud and rolled onto her side on the sofa.

"Tutored?" I asked.

Rachel looked down at her feet. "Sorta."

I took another deep breath and tried to relax. "Look, Linc is missing. I'm trying to find him. He's not in trouble. And I don't care about the pot or anything else you two probably have stashed in here. Just be straight with me."

It was quiet for a moment while they tried to process what I'd said.

"Just tell him," Dana finally said.

"Shut up," Rachel said, looking at her.

"He's not from the school," Dana said, frowning at her friend. Then she looked at me. "Right? You aren't some kinda school cop?"

"I'm not."

She looked back at Rachel. "See?"

Rachel frowned at her friend, but didn't say anything.

Dana turned back to me. "Linc wrote papers for her."

"Dana! Shut up!" Rachel said, her cheeks flushing slightly.

"And she fucked him in return," Dana said, smiling.

"You bitch," Rachel said, shaking her head.

College had apparently changed since I'd been enrolled.

"It wasn't just like that," Rachel said to me.

"Okay," I said. "I'm not looking for an explanation. I just want to find him."

Rachel's cheeks continued to flush. "I mean, I can't write very good. He offered to help. And it just kinda . . . happened."

"Just once?"

Dana laughed.

"Well, no," Rachel said. "A couple times. But not recently. The last time was like two months ago. I swear."

"Okay. When did you see him last?"

She thought about it, lines forming above her perfect eyebrows. "Two days ago."

"Any idea where he might be?"

She shook her head slowly. "No. Do you think he's in trouble?"

"No idea," I said, wishing I hadn't knocked on their door. I pulled a card from my pocket and held it out. "If you hear from him or think of anything, call me."

Dana lurched off the sofa. "Can I get one of those?"

I reluctantly withdrew another one and handed it to her.

She smiled at it, then winked at me. "Thanks, stud."

I left before my head exploded.

3

I walked out to the parking lot to find a scowling, heavyset man next to my Jeep.

He was looking into the driver's-side window, a Louisville Slugger dangling from his right hand.

"Need a ride?" I asked.

He turned around. About five-eight with more than his share of weight around his gut and his neck, rings of sweat staining the armpits of his gray T-shirt. The brown hair on his head was almost gone. Sweat beaded down his wrinkled forehead into his small, dark eyes. A flat nose and a crooked mouth didn't improve his appearance.

"You a friend of that kid's?" he said, raising the bat up and pointing in the direction of Linc's apartment.

"No."

"Then why were you at his door?"

"Why do you care?"

The small eyes narrowed. "You getting smart with me?"

"I was smart before I got here."

He looked confused.

"I'm not a friend of his," I told him. "I've never met him. I'm looking for him."

The man relaxed and lowered the bat to his side. "You and me both."

"I'm Noah," I said, offering my hand.

He shook it, leaving a film of perspiration on my palm. "Sam Rolovich. Kid owes me rent."

I casually wiped my hand against my shorts. "You the super?"

He frowned, like I'd insulted him. "Property manager."

"Sorry. He owes you?"

He nodded, glancing up at the apartment. "Two months' worth." His eyes shifted and he was looking at me with suspicion. "Why do you care?"

I pulled a card out of my pocket and handed it to him. "Linc's brother asked me to help him find him."

He studied the card. "Hmm. A private eye. For real?"

"For real."

"Never met one of you before."

"Right. The rent thing—is that a regular deal for him?"

"No," Sam said, hitching up his jeans with his free hand, exposing decade-old flip-flops on his feet. "Kid's lived here a year and always paid ahead a time. Last month, he gave me some story about having to pay tuition, said he was gonna be late." He shrugged. "Me, I'm a nice guy, so I let it slide. I know where he lives, you know?"

Sam looked like anything but a nice guy, but I played along. "Sure."

"So, then when I didn't get this month's rent on Friday, I came looking for him. He wasn't there. Then his brother showed up and said he didn't know where he was, either. Promised to find him." He frowned and wiped the sweat from his forehead. "Haven't seen the kid or his friends yet."

I nodded at the bat. "Maybe he's scared."

Sam looked at the bat, then looked embarrassed. "Hey, you never know who you're gonna run into."

So true.

"You said friends. I thought he lived by himself."

He made a face and the crooked mouth got more crooked. "He does, but all those fucking bangers are always hanging around with him."

"Bangers? As in gangbangers?" I said, not sure I'd heard him correctly.

He nodded. "Yep. One of them used to live here, but I kicked his ass out. Got tired of all the bullshit."

"Remember his name?"

A plane roared over us, headed to Lindbergh, the engines quickly fading in the distance.

He pointed toward the office. "Come on. Let's go take a look."

I followed him to a door just off the side of the building. The room was about the size of a small closet. An old wooden desk sat in the middle, surrounded by two metal filing cabinets and two metal folding chairs. The desk was covered in piles of paper and manila folders. A calendar with a busty woman in a bikini leaning over the hood of a car hung on the wall behind the desk. An aroma of old popcorn and stale beer clung to the air.

"Have a seat," Sam said, waving at one of the chairs. He stood the bat up next to one of the cabinets. "Ignore the mess."

I wasn't sure what my other choice was, so I didn't say anything.

He opened up the middle drawer on one of the cabinets and rummaged through it for a moment, then yanked out a thin red folder.

"Here it is," he said, turning around and sitting down in the chair on the other side of the desk. "Fucker's name was Deacon Moreno." He handed the file across the desk to me.

The photocopied driver's license photo showed a young black man with a hard face. No smile, no trace of humor in his expression. His date of birth put him at twenty-four years old. Six-foot and 185 pounds. The address listed was in Logan Heights, a neighborhood even I wouldn't venture into alone.

"The address on the license was bogus," Sam said. "He owed me rent. I went to collect but it's a laundromat."

I handed the folder back to Sam. "Why'd you kick him out?"

"Oh, man," he said, rolling his eyes. "That guy was a problem from the day he walked in. Late with his rent, that goddamned hip-hop music booming out of his place and car at all hours, all his hotshot homeboys hanging out in the parking lot all the time."

"How did you know they were gang members?"

He rolled his eyes again. "Come on. What am I, an idiot? Bunch of fucking black kids in tricked-out cars, wearing Raiders jerseys and gold chains, smoking weed." He tapped his temple with his index finger. "I know because I know."

I wasn't so sure. There was a big difference between kids who acted like gangsters and those who actually lived the life. But I didn't want to insult Sam's astute observations. Afraid he might show me his white hood and cross-burning tools.

"And after you evicted Deacon, he came to see Linc?" I asked.

"Yep. Couple of times. Him and some of his buddies. Usually at night."

The picture I was getting of Linc was far from the one his brother had drawn for me. Trading sex for homework wasn't the most ethical thing, but I could see where a guy his age would consider an offer like that from an attractive girl like Rachel. A serious kid who was trying to get his degree, though, didn't run with a gang or store guns in his apartment. Falling in with a bad crowd was one thing. Falling in with a gang was another.

"How about the girls that live next door to Linc?" I asked.

Sam laughed. "The stoner chicks? No problems with them. One of their rich daddies pays for them. Two months at a time. They don't bother me."

The unmistakable sound of a gunshot outside froze us.

Sam stood up. "What the fuck?"

Tires squealed on pavement. I jumped up from the chair and shoved the door open to the parking lot.

The lot was empty save for my Jeep. I looked to the street and saw traffic moving at a normal pace. I looked back toward the apartments.

Rachel was standing outside her door. Her left hand was against the wall, bracing herself, and her eyes were wide, confused, and frightened. Her right hand was at her chest, blood spilling out over her fingers.

Sam burst out of the office behind me, the bat in his hand.

"Go call nine-one-one," I told him.

But he didn't move.

We both stood there and watched Rachel crumple to the ground.

4

Detective John Wellton said, "Braddock. What a complete and utterly unpleasant surprise."

We were standing in the parking lot and I watched as the EMTs loaded Rachel into the ambulance, ready to take her to Sharp Hospital. She'd been shot once. There was a lot of blood and I couldn't tell how badly she was hurt.

"I'm missing a gnome in my garden," I said. "You'd make a nice replacement."

Wellton glared at me. He wore a light blue oxford open at the neck tucked into gray dress slacks. The sunglasses on his face were just slightly darker than his skin. And even in the thick-heeled loafers, he didn't break five-four.

"Funny, asshole." He turned back to the apartments. "What did you see?"

I watched a team of officers mill around the spot where she'd been shot. "Came out of the office. She was already standing there. Then she collapsed."

He nodded and removed the sunglasses. "See the shooter?"

"Nope. I heard the shot, but that was it." I pointed at Sam's office. "I was in there."

He nodded again. We watched Dana come out of the apartment with two officers. She was sobbing and each officer had an arm under an elbow to keep her steady.

"And your reason for being here?" Wellton asked.

"Is none of your business," I said.

He snorted. "Well, whatever you were doing, nice work."

I hadn't seen him in a while and he was as irritating as I remembered.

"I was looking for the kid that lives in the apartment next to hers," I said, deciding there was no reason to keep it from him. "Talked to both girls for maybe ten minutes, they didn't know anything about where he is. Then I came out and talked to the manager."

I thought about the guns that Peter had seen in Linc's apartment. I hadn't seen them yet, so I wasn't sure they existed. At least, that's how I rationalized not bringing them up.

"Rolovich is the manager?"

"Yeah. A piece of crap, but I don't think he knows anything."

"You two probably had a lot in common, then."

Maybe Wellton was more irritating than I remembered.

"Santangelo should be here in a minute," he said, glancing at me.

My stomach tightened at the mention of his partner's name. I hadn't seen her in a while and I didn't have any plans to change that.

"She's coming down?" I asked.

He looked at his watch. "Anytime now."

A knot. It was now a definite knot in my stomach.

"You done with me?" I asked.

Wellton turned to me, his eyes steady. "Still on the outs with her, huh?"

"Wouldn't know. Haven't spoken to her in a long time."

"Lucky her," he said, the corners of his mouth flickering into a grin. "Yeah, I'm done with you. For now."

"Can I take my Jeep?"

He smiled and shook his head. "That I'm not done with."

"Why not?"

"It's inside my crime scene."

"When can I get it back?"

His smile got bigger. "When I say so." He paused. "Maybe I'll take it for a spin."

"You should. It's probably more fun than your Big Wheel."

His smile disappeared. He glared at me for a moment, then turned and moved away.

I walked to the street and stood there, wondering how I was going to get home. I was contemplating the bus when a Yellow Cab came down El Cajon. I waved at him and he came over three lanes to meet me.

"Where to?" he asked out the passenger window, leaning across the passenger seat.

"Mission Beach."

"You got cash?"

"Yeah."

"All yours, then."

As I opened the rear passenger door, I glanced up and saw Liz Santangelo stepping out of her car on the far side of the lot.

She shut the door and stood next to the car. She wore a bright green blouse and slim black pants. Her dark hair was pulled back over her shoulders and I could make out silver earrings on her ears. Her gun bulged on her hip.

I hadn't seen her in about six months. The last time I'd seen her had been in a hospital hallway. She'd walked out on me, disappointed again in a choice I'd made, our always-sputtering relationship screeching to a halt. I'd done something impulsive against her wishes that had resulted in the deaths of two people and nearly mine as well.

I hadn't called her and she hadn't called me. My reason was stubbornness. I wasn't sure what hers was.

But seeing her now, I realized how much I missed her.

She glanced in my direction, doing a double-take, and then the look on her face telling me that she wished she hadn't done that. Or that she at least wished I hadn't seen her do it.

We stood there for a moment, each of us looking at the other, she looking as unsure as I felt.

I finally held my hand up to Liz, a halfhearted, confused wave. Maybe a symbolic white flag of sorts.

She blinked once, turned her head, and walked over

to the group of cops in the parking lot without acknowledging me.

"We going anytime soon, pal?" the driver asked from inside the idling cab.

I slid into the backseat, stung more than I wanted to be. "Yeah. We're going right now."

5

The cab dropped me off at the corner of Mission and Jamaica. Mission Beach is a conglomeration of maze-like alleys about ten feet wide and I didn't want to subject him to the rigors of maneuvering to my house.

I grabbed a beer out of the fridge and heard clapping out near my patio. I walked out of the kitchen and opened the back slider.

Carter, all six-foot-nine of him, was doing a handstand on the three-foot wall that separates my patio from the boardwalk. A group of four Japanese tourists were alternately snapping photos of him and cheering from the boardwalk side of the wall.

"Did you tell them that you can drink beer through your nose, too?" I asked.

He lifted his head in my direction. "I didn't think they'd find that as charming."

He brought his legs down and sprang off the wall onto the patio, his yellow board shorts and white tank top falling into place. His fans erupted into more applause.

He bowed to them and held out his hand. They shoved some cash into his massive palm and then shuffled off, chattering excitedly among themselves.

"Do I get a cut of that?" I asked, sitting down in one of the patio chairs.

"No."

"It's my property."

He shoved the bills into his pocket and grinned. "Yeah, but you don't support my act."

"That is so true."

Carter Hamm, my best friend, sat down next to me. His white-blond hair was sticking up like tiny spikes on his head. He propped his huge feet up on the small table in front of us.

"That dude find you this morning?" he asked.

I looked across the boardwalk to where Peter Pluto had waited for me at the edge of the water. "Yeah. Let's chat about that."

"Chat? You must really be pissed."

"Handstands and perceptive. You are one of a kind."

He leaned back in the chair. "That's what the ladies tell me."

I sipped from the beer and shook my head. "Yeah, the dude from this morning found me. When I was out in the water. When I wasn't looking for a job."

Carter glanced to me, his dark eyes squinting into the disappearing sun. "So you bailed on him?"

I took another drink and didn't say anything.

"No, of course not," he said, nodding his head. "You decided to help him. Plus, you need cash."

"It's your fault."

"Is not."

"Is too."

"I just told him where to find you."

"And you knew I'd say yes."

"I didn't even know what he wanted."

"Not to take my picture doing a handstand, that's for sure."

"Well, you suck at handstands."

Arguing with Carter was like arguing with a three-year-old—a genetic freak of a three-year-old.

I held up my hand. "Fine. My fault."

He folded his arms across his chest and nodded. "Exactly. So what happened?"

"Went to look for this guy's brother at his apartment and while I was there, a girl got shot."

"Shut up."

"I'd like to, but you keep asking me questions."

I set my beer down on the table between our chairs. He immediately snatched it, held it up to his mouth, and emptied it.

"Tell me," he said, setting the empty bottle down.

I told him about Linc's place, the girls, Rolovich, and the shooting.

"That's some afternoon," he said when I was done.

"No kidding."

"You gonna keep looking for the kid?"

I shrugged because I didn't know now if I wanted to or not.

We sat there staring for a few minutes at the bouquet of purples and yellows in the sky at the far edge of the water. The crowd on the boardwalk was slowly dissipating as the evening trudged in.

"You wanna go out?" Carter asked, gesturing at the water. "Decent swells should be here soon."

I closed my eyes. "Nah."

We sat there again quietly for a few moments.

"You saw her, didn't you?" he said finally.

"Saw who?"

"The Virgin Mary. Who the hell do you think I mean? Liz."

I didn't say anything. Of all the annoying things about Carter, perhaps the one that bugged me the most was his ability to read me like an eye chart.

"Did you talk to her?" he asked.

"Nope."

"Why not?"

"Didn't feel like it."

"Right."

The truth was I didn't know why I hadn't just gone over to talk to Liz. Maybe it was because I was afraid of what she'd say to me. Not talking to her had become weirdly comfortable and I wasn't sure I was ready to give that up.

Carter stood, yanked off his tank top, and grabbed the eight-foot G&S surfboard next to the sliding door. He tucked it under his arm and stepped over the small stone wall onto the boardwalk.

He turned around. "You know I can't stand her, dude. I really can't. It would be fine with me if I never saw her again, never had to hear her name again." He shook his head. "But if you're in love with her, or whatever, you're just being chickenshit. Flat out. So she's pissed at you. Big deal. Liz is pissed at everyone, as far as I can tell. Deal with it and quit sulking. I've watched it for too long now and I'm tired of it." He shook his head. "I've never thought of you as a coward, Noah, and I don't really wanna start."

He turned and walked down the sand toward the water and the exploding hues of the horizon and left me to think about that.

6

After a night of restless sleep, Rachel's eyes, Liz's face, and Carter's words rattling around in my brain, I decided I needed a few more details from Peter Pluto. I needed to see what specifically he'd meant by maybe Linc getting hooked up with a bad crowd. Did he know about the gang or was there another crowd I needed to be aware of?

And as much as I wanted to avoid the subject, I wanted to know more about their father. Nothing he'd told me about his brother had added up and I ended up watching a girl I'd just met take a bullet. I didn't know whether the shooting was tied directly to Linc Pluto's disappearance, but it sure seemed like an awfully big coincidence.

I walked up Mission to the Enterprise rental office, and after fifteen minutes drove away in a rented Ford Taurus. My car was still impounded and I didn't mind sticking a few more dollars on Peter Pluto's tab.

His home was in Clairemont, a nondescript suburb north of the downtown area and twenty minutes from my house. The community rests on the hills just above Mission Bay and stretches two dozen miles to the east. Middle-class housing, strip malls, and neighborhoods that had deteriorated marked what had once been a desired address. Most of the original residents had vacated to the sprawling suburbs of the east and north, seeking newer homes and newer schools, leaving most of Clairemont in search of an identity.

His address was just off Balboa, in the Mount streets, so named because the streets were named after the mountains of the world. I turned right on Mt. Arafat and then right again on Mt. Everest.

Not something you do every day.

I found Pluto's house near the end of a cul-de-sac on Mt. Everest. The ranch home was a faded gray, with a giant plum tree in the front yard. A beat-up basketball hoop rested above the garage and the grass in the yard was a mix of green and brown. A bright blue Ford pickup was parked in the driveway.

I walked up the drive to find both the screen door and front door wide open.

I poked my head in the entryway. "Hello?"

No one responded. I stepped onto the small tiled area just inside the door.

The living room had been ransacked. A TV was on the carpeting, smashed to pieces. The furniture was flipped over, pushed into a pile in the middle of the room.

I turned to the dining room. The table was dumped on its side, the oak chairs splintered into jagged hunks of wood. An overhead light had been yanked off the ceiling and crushed into glass shards.

My heart picked up speed.

Someone had issues with Peter Pluto's house.

I heard footsteps down the hallway off the dining room and stepped back, reaching for my gun, then realizing it was stuck in the glove box, impounded with my Jeep.

A guy somewhere in his twenties with a shaved head emerged. He was about my height at six-three, but thicker. He wore a gray T-shirt, dirty jeans, and scuffed black boots. The scowl on his face didn't detract from the quarter-sized black swastika tattooed just above his left eyebrow.

He paused when he saw me, then took a step in my direction. "Who the fuck are you?"

"That was gonna be my question for you."

The scowl on his face tightened and I noticed what looked like blood on the knuckles of his right hand.

He took another step toward me, his small eyes narrowing. "You fuckin' with me?"

I held up my hands. "Just wondering if you were the one who did the redecorating in here."

He stared at me for a moment, completely unafraid and completely angry. He glanced down the hallway from where he'd come, then back at me. His expression slowly changed. The snarl morphed into an arrogant, evil grin exposing yellow teeth. He shook his head. "Dude, you walked into the wrong house."

Not the wrong house, but maybe the wrong time. "Did I?"

He laughed, as if I didn't realize how stupid I actually was. "Yeah, you did. Wanna tell me why you're here?"

"Not really."

He shook his head again. "I'm not asking, dude. Why you here?"

He looked meaner than me, a veteran of fights that he'd probably instigated. But he was younger, which meant he wasn't wiser.

I followed his lead and stepped toward him. "Tell you what. Before I kick your ass and call the cops, why don't you tell me why *you're* here?"

His eyes flared and he stepped forward, a right hook coming at my head. I stepped inside of it and jammed the heel of my hand into his jaw. He fell backward against the wall of the dining room and slumped to the floor.

I stood over him for a moment. He refocused his eyes and brought his hand to his mouth, a thick stream of blood now coming out onto his chin.

"You done talking back now?" I asked him.

He looked at the blood on his hand, then at me. The slow, ugly grin came back, his teeth now red rather than yellow. "Yeah, I guess I am." He looked past me and lifted his chin. "Mo's gonna take over."

I turned around and after getting a look at the guy, I just assumed Mo was short for Mountain.

He was about six-foot-seven and a minimum of three hundred pounds of muscle. His nose was so crooked, it had to have been broken half a dozen times in half a dozen places. His gray eyes were empty, just staring at me. He wore a thick silver hoop in each ear. The dirty white tank top on his body exposed arms that were covered completely in tattoos. Women, birds, and swords, from what I could make out. His black jeans were torn in multiple places and the toes of his construction boots were caked in blood.

His head was also shaved and the phrase WHITE IS RIGHT was tattooed just above his forehead in simple black letters.

He looked around me at his partner. "You alright, Lonnie?"

"I'm fine," Lonnie said from behind me.

"Want me to hurt him?" Mo asked, much in the same way one would ask if you needed a ride somewhere.

"Yep."

I didn't like the way my future was being discussed without my involvement. I wasn't scared of Lonnie, but Mo looked less than human and I didn't see a way out of this.

"He see anything?" Mo asked, still looking around me.

"Don't think so. Make sure it stays that way."

Mo gave a quick nod and moved at me faster than I expected. His right hand grasped my forearm and he pulled me forward. His left fist crashed into my stomach like a battering ram. Every ounce of air exploded from my body. The battering ram reloaded and slammed into my temple, an ugly rainbow of colors exploding in the backs of my eyes. I felt my knees buckle, but his hold on my forearm kept me up.

Lonnie walked around behind Mo, showing me another bloody grin. "Now you wanna tell me what you're here for?"

A wave of nausea swept through my body as Mo held me up like a rag doll. I knew I was in trouble, but there was no way I was giving in to some racist punk.

"Fuck you," I managed, trying to ready myself for what I knew was coming.

"You a friend of Pete's?" Lonnie asked.

I didn't answer.

"How about his little brother, the missing Linc?" he asked, grinning at me.

I looked away from him and tried to catch my breath.

Lonnie's smile changed to a frown. "You came here for a reason. What was it?"

I turned back to him. "Fuck you some more."

Lonnie backed up, then kicked me in the stomach and the air rushed out of me again. Mo held me up.

"You don't wanna talk now?" Lonnie said, moving toward me. "That's cool. I'm gonna have my man Mo work you over a little bit. Not kill you. Just make you wish he had. But I need to know why you showed up here today, man. So when you wake up . . . if you wake up . . . think about me. Because I'll be around. And the next time you see me?" He leaned closer. "You'll be too scared to tell me to fuck off. And that's when you'll tell me what you were here for. And that's when I'll kill you, asshole." He looked at Mo. "Have at him, dude."

Mo spun me around and stared at me with the same empty look. His fist crashed into my temple again and my legs gave way completely. He tossed me to the ground, my face smashing into the carpet.

Lonnie leaned down over me, his breath warm and foul. "Don't fuck with us, dude. Not ever. You can't win." I could feel him right next to my ear. "And remember. Next time, you talk and then you die."

I groaned and rolled over on my back. Lonnie stepped away and Mo took his place, blocking out everything behind him. He knelt down beside me and pulled back his fist, ready to drop the battering ram once again on my face.

I turned away, as if doing so might protect me, and my eyes locked on something at the end of the hallway from where Lonnie had first emerged.

As Mo prepared to put me to sleep, I hoped that I would live to remember seeing what appeared to be Peter Pluto's body at the end of the hallway.

7

Warm dirt pressed against my face. Blood pooled in my mouth. My body throbbed. I felt tired, like I hadn't slept in days. I slowly forced one eye open.

Sunlight glared against the brush.

Everything was sideways.

Where was I?

I coughed, spasms of pain ricocheting through my stomach and back, and spit out a mouthful of blood. I lifted my head, needing to see where I was. My neck shivered as it tried to support the weight.

Tumbleweeds. Dirt. Gravel. The desert?

I laid my head down again, the ground hot and rough against my cheek. The warmth of the ground made me want to close my eyes and go back to sleep.

I lifted my head again and twisted in the other direction.

More dried brush, more tumbleweeds, a body.

I twisted my torso in that direction.

I heard someone scream, the noise echoing in the distance, and realized it was me.

I got my elbows beneath me and pushed up and felt myself start to slide backward.

I was on a slope.

Slopes in the desert didn't make any sense to me. Nothing made sense.

I stabbed my toes into the ground to stop the sliding.

Focusing on the body, I crawled toward it on my elbows, up the slope. My legs were stiff and heavy and I couldn't get them to bend.

The body was only about ten feet away, but it felt like a hundred. My elbows ached. And bled. Nausea worked its way through my body like a current.

I laid my head down again, listening to my gasps for air. Everything was spinning slowly.

I forced my head up again.

Peter Pluto looked back at me, his eyes empty and his face devoid of any life.

I dropped my head down on the earth again and wondered if I was about to join him.

8

I tried to raise my eyelids, but they felt like they were sealed shut with concrete. My head pounded. I was on my back and I could feel my arms and legs, but they felt four times heavier than they should have.

I squeezed my eyes shut, then forced them to open slightly.

The bright lights of the hospital room shocked me and I shut my eyes again.

At least the son of a bitch hadn't killed me.

I heard movement to my left and I rotated my head in that direction, the muscles in my neck feeling like taut rubber bands. I got my eyes half open.

Liz was sitting in a chair, looking at me.

"You awake?" she asked.

I opened my mouth, but nothing came out. I swallowed hard and wondered who placed the invisible boulder on my chest.

I tried again. "Yeah." My voice sounded distant and old.

"You don't sound like it."

I turned my head back to stare at the ceiling. "Awake. Not alive."

"You're in the hospital," she said. "Mission Bay."

"Okay."

"You've been here about twelve hours."

That surprised me, because it felt like just minutes before that Mo had been planting his fists into my body and I'd been lying somewhere with Peter Pluto.

I looked back at Liz. She wore her black running tights, a blue sweatshirt, and Nike running shoes. Her dark hair was pulled back in a ponytail.

"You find me?" I asked, my voice coming back closer to my head now. I fumbled with the glass of water I'd noticed next to my bed and took a long drink.

She shook her head. "No. Couple of kids stumbled across you in a canyon in Clairemont."

Not the desert. A canyon. That explained the slope.

My head felt puffy. I set the glass back on the table and looked at my arms. No tubes or wires hooked into me.

"They just beat the crap out of you," she said. "No broken bones, no real bleeding. They knew what they were doing."

I had learned that the hard way.

She leaned back in the chair. "What happened, Noah?"

I stared at the ceiling again, trying to gain some focus. Lonnie's words were ringing in my ears. He wanted me to wake up. He wanted me to hurt. And he wanted me to feel afraid.

He won.

I closed my eyes.

"I've sat here for six hours," Liz said. "Call came in to Wellton, he called me. Not because I was on duty, but because he thought I'd want to know. I hate that he was right, but he was." She paused and folded her arms across her chest. "I've sat here, looking at you, worrying about you, trying to figure out why. I haven't figured it out yet. And I don't know if I'm going to. Ever. But there's no way you're going to lie there and not talk to me." She bit her bottom lip for a moment. "So tell me what happened, Noah, because if you don't, I am done wasting another second of my life thinking about you."

"Christ, Liz," I said, my tongue feeling lost in my mouth. "I'm trying to clear my head. Give me a second."

I opened my eyes and kept them on the white ceiling, feeling the pangs in my chest each time I exhaled. I remembered her looking away from me at the apartment building.

"I thought you already were done with me anyway," I said, looking at her.

She shifted in her chair, then glanced over me to the window. "I'm not here to talk about us. Now's not the time."

"Why not?"

"Because if we try that, I'd probably end up kicking your ass and I think you've had all you can handle for now."

I wasn't sure if it was what had happened to me or if it was just being near her again, but the ice had been broken on the freeze-out between us and I wanted it to continue to melt away.

"When's the time gonna come, then?" I asked. "For us?"

She moved her gaze from the window to me. "I don't know. I'm not sure it will."

I stared at her for a moment, then went back to concentrating on the ceiling.

"Huge," I finally said.

"What?"

"He was huge."

"Who?"

"Mo."

"Who's Mo?"

"The mountain that fell on me."

I told her about working for Peter Pluto, what I remembered about going to the house, about finding Lonnie and then Mo finding me.

"Skinheads?" she asked after I told her about the tattoos.

I tried to nod, but it came off more like a spasm. "Hard-core. Aryan Nations stuff." I cleared my throat and tried to get my voice to sound normal. "I think they killed Pluto."

Liz stood and came over to the edge of the bed. "They found a body with yours. No ID."

The memory of crawling up next to him was still hazy, but I'd recognized him. "That was him."

She nodded. "I'll get John the name and we'll check

on next of kin. You know if this Peter Pluto was into that racist crap?"

"I don't know," I said.

"Well, let me know if you hear anything," she said, as she came over and sat on the edge of the bed, careful not to jostle me. "You're gonna be okay."

I looked away from her and toward the window on the other side of the room. "Yep."

"None of it's permanent. You're gonna hurt like hell, but it'll go away."

I nodded. I knew that. It was the mental part that I had questions about. I couldn't help wondering if I could've done something to avoid it all. Not taken the case, not gone to the house, not gone in without a gun. But all of those were things I normally did. I didn't want to change because of this, alter the way I thought and the way I acted. But through all the pain I could feel something shifting in me, a combination of fear and anger that was shifting even as I tried to stop it.

"I called Carter a little bit ago. Didn't know who else to call," Liz said. "Got his voice mail, told him you were here."

"Thanks."

She stood up and I could feel her eyes on me. "I'm gonna go."

I turned to her. "Okay. Thanks. For coming."

"I'll check on you in a couple of days." She hesitated for a moment, then touched my hand quickly, covering it with hers. "There's something else, though, Noah."

"What?"

"You have your ID with you when you went in?"

I thought about it. "Yeah. My wallet. In the pocket of my shorts."

Liz nodded. "I figured. But it wasn't on you." She paused. "They probably took it. Most likely for the money or credit cards."

I knew what she was getting at. "But they know where I live."

"If they wanted to know, yeah, they do now."

It didn't surprise me, but hearing it out loud made my stomach jolt.

"We found your rental, too," she said. "Up in University City, a little beat-up. I'm gonna talk to John and I'll get your Jeep back to your place tomorrow."

A tiny, selfish voice popped into my head. The guy who was supposed to pay me and for that rental car was dead. A couple of days in the hospital were sure to jack up my insurance premium. Money was the last thing I wanted to think about, but the concern was there like a fly that wouldn't die.

"Okay," I said.

"I'll be in touch," Liz said, giving my hand a quick squeeze, then heading for the door. "I'm glad you're alright."

I didn't know that I really was, but I watched her go without saying anything, as the fear and anger in my body and in my thoughts continued to work themselves together in a gathering fury that I wasn't sure how to handle.

9

A nurse came in bright and early the next morning and woke me up to inform me that since there was nothing further they could do for me, I was on my way out. She assured me I'd be fine and said she'd be back shortly with some papers that needed my signature.

Gee, thanks.

The pain had kept me awake for parts of the night. My limbs were heavy and sore and my chest felt like a tractor had been parked on it. When I was finally able to get myself out of bed to use the bathroom, my back cracked and burned the more I tried to straighten it.

The mirror in the bathroom told the same story. The circles around my eyes were a myriad of reds and purples. I had a huge split in my bottom lip and more bruises on each cheek.

The nurse returned and I signed the discharge papers, refused the wheelchair trip out, and was pulling on my clothes from the closet when Carter walked into the room. He wore brown board shorts and a bright purple T-shirt. He looked out of breath.

"Sorry," he said, frowning. "I was in LA."

"It's alright."

"I just checked my voice mail this morning," he said. "I came as soon as I listened to Liz's message."

"It's alright."

"I'm really sorry, Noah."

It wasn't like him to offer sincere, direct apologies. I knew my appearance probably rattled him.

I pulled on my shorts and T-shirt, trying not to grimace. "Dude. It's okay. I haven't been much fun anyway."

"Still. Shoulda been here."

"Whatever." I stepped into my sandals. "You can make it up to me by getting me out of here."

He nodded and opened the door.

We walked silently out of the hospital and I was so glad to breathe fresh air that I didn't make my usual remark about his god-awful-looking car. The topless Dodge Ram Charger, painted like a zebra, save for the skull on the hood, was a welcome sight.

We made it to my place in fifteen minutes. My Jeep was out front like Liz had promised. Carter stood awkwardly next to the car, not sure how to help me. I waved him off and struggled out, figuring the movement would keep me from getting stiff.

By the time I made it to my sofa, I was winded.

Carter went to the fridge, opened two Coronas, and came around to the couch. He placed one on the table in front of me.

"Thanks," I said, reaching for it, deciding I'd substitute the alcohol for the pain pills I'd been prescribed.

He nodded and took a long pull from his bottle. He set the bottle down and took a deep breath.

"So," he said. "Anybody we know?"

I took a drink from the bottle, the beer tasting much better than the water and juice I'd been given in the hospital. I shook my head. "Don't think so."

"But you'll know them when you see them?"

"Oh, yeah."

"Good. You say when and we'll put them down. I'll call in a few favors." He drank from the beer again. "You can be in on it or not. I don't care. But these fuckers are going down."

I nodded and didn't say anything. I wasn't sure if I wanted in on it. I wasn't sure if I ever wanted to see their faces again. And that bothered me more than anything else.

I changed the subject. "Why were you in LA?"

He smiled and pointed the bottle in my direction. "Workin' on a real job."

"No. Seriously."

"Workin', dude."

"A real job?"

He shrugged his massive shoulders. "Yeah, I guess. I'm gonna be on TV."

I leaned back in the sofa. "Excuse me?"

He drained the beer and set the empty bottle on the table. "Acting."

"So, while I was in the hospital, hell froze over?"

"Funny. I'm gonna be a reenactment actor."

"A what?"

His eyebrows danced over his eyes, the excitement apparent. "Okay, you know like *America's Most Wanted* and shows like that?"

"Um, yeah."

"Well, they do reenactments of the crimes they're trying to solve. I'm gonna play the bad guy in a couple of reenactments. Wear a wife-beater tank top and everything."

I stared at him for a moment, then started laughing. "You've found your calling."

He nodded, proud. "It's not for sure yet, but who knows? This could lead to movie roles or some shit like that."

I held the beer up. "Who knows?"

"So, anyway, I may be spending a little time up there in the next couple weeks." He paused and looked at me. "But not until you're alright."

"I'm alright now," I said.

"Sure," he said, but I could tell he didn't believe me.

I shifted uncomfortably on the sofa. I didn't want anyone feeling sorry for me or seeing the embarrassment and fear I didn't seem to be able to put to bed. And I didn't want anyone but Mo and Lonnie on the receiving end of my anger.

I pushed myself off the sofa and walked over to the corner of the room where my surfboards stood. I moved the six-foot Ron Jon off to the side and put my hands on the nine-foot Merrick that hadn't seen the ocean in a while.

"You thinking of hitting the water?" Carter asked.

"Yeah. Probably won't even ride. Just sit out there."

"Cool. I'll go with you."

I turned around. "No. I'm gonna go out by myself."

Carter looked at me, a little unsure and skeptical. "You sure? You still look a little wobbly."

I nodded and pulled the board away from the wall. "Yeah. I just need some air, some space, you know? I'm just gonna get out there and watch."

"You want me to wait here? Make sure you can make it back okay?"

I shook my head. "I don't need a babysitter."

"Not what I meant, Noah."

"I know."

I'd taken a beating like this once before, courtesy of a drug lord I'd pissed off. The difference then, though, was that I knew it was coming. This one had blindsided me. I just wanted to get away from everyone who knew what had happened. I wanted to hide so I wouldn't have to explain anything to anyone. The bruises would heal, the pain would go away, but I wasn't sure how to fix the worry and rage that had taken up residence in my head.

I opened the screen door to the patio and laid the board outside in the bright afternoon sunlight. I grabbed the long-sleeved red rash guard off the back of the lounge chair, pulled off my T-shirt, and struggled to get the guard on over my head. I knew that I looked awkward getting it on, my arms still a little uncoordinated, and that the bruises on my body gave the impression that someone had splashed me with purple paint, but Carter didn't say anything.

"I just wanna be alone for a while, okay?" I said finally.

Carter stood up off the sofa. "Okay."

I shut the screen door. I picked up the board and stepped over the short wall to the boardwalk.

"Noah."

I turned around. Carter was standing at the screen door.

"It would've happened to whoever walked into that house," he said. "Me, you, Mike Tyson. Wouldn't have mattered. You weren't expecting it. No one would've been ready for that."

I shifted the board under my arm. "I know."

He tilted his head slightly. "Do you? Really?"

I turned and walked down the sand toward the shimmering water, unable to answer that question.

10

I sat out on my board, just beyond the break, for about an hour. I moved out to the side of the lineup, ignoring the looks I was getting from the others out on the water when they took in my appearance, just watching and resting. The water and air felt good on my body and it gave me a chance to clear my head. By the time I paddled in, I felt better.

I spent the rest of the day napping and watching television. Every couple of hours, I'd walk outside and do some stretches on the patio, trying to make sure nothing stayed locked up. The stretching hurt, but I knew it would pay off in the next couple of days.

After a night of sleep and a slow morning walk on the beach to loosen my muscles, I called Mike Berkley and arranged to meet him downtown after his workday ended. I figured I needed to do a little backtracking. Peter Pluto had said that Mike had given him my name, so he seemed a logical place to start.

I ate lunch, paid a few bills, and took another brisk stroll on the sand before making the twenty-minute drive down I-5 to the west end of the downtown area to meet Mike. I parked at the corner of Ash and Columbia and took a quick glance at myself in the rearview mirror. The bruising on my face seemed to be less pronounced, but there was no denying that I looked like a raccoon. At least I was downtown, where sights like my face might blend in.

Mike had suggested meeting at the Columbia Street Brewery and, as the name indicated, it was on Columbia Street. Situated between several of the newer skyscrapers to creep up the downtown San Diego landscape, it was an after-hours hot spot.

The interior consisted of oak, brass, and glass. The giant mirrors on the walls made the interior look twice as large as it actually was. The restaurant area was pushed off to the left, tables nearly stacked on top of one another to accommodate the growing crowd. The bar ran lengthwise down the right side, bartenders in T-shirts and jeans scurrying back and forth behind it.

I hesitated in the entryway, scanning the crowd. As my eyes panned across the room, I realized I wasn't just looking for Mike. My brain was keeping an eye out for Lonnie and Mo, as well. It was silly to think they'd be at this kind of place, but the beating had put me on full alert.

I found Mike at the far end of the bar. He was loosening the blue and red tie from the collar on his white oxford. He glanced at me, looked away for a second, then whipped back in my direction.

His eyes widened as I approached.

"What the fuck happened to you?" he asked.

"Hazard of the job," I said, extending my hand and avoiding an explanation.

He shook it and nodded at the stool next to him. "Sit down before I have to pick you up."

"I'm okay."

He looked at me. His light brown hair was cut close to his head. His eye color matched the hair and his complexion was vibrant and tan, not something you usually see on an attorney who spends a lot of time in his office. He was a couple of years older than me and I hadn't seen him in a few months, but every time I saw him, he seemed to get younger.

"You seriously alright?" he asked.

"Fine."

Mike stared at me for a second, then shrugged. He waved at the bartender, pointed at his beer and then the empty space in front of me.

"Thanks for meeting me," I said after the beer arrived.

"Hey. Thanks for coming here," he said. "I'm meeting a date here in a little bit."

"Don't let me get in the way."

He grinned, exposing bright white teeth. "Don't worry. I won't."

Mike lived a serious bachelor's life and liked it that way. His good looks, charm, and wit made it easy for him.

I took a drink from the beer and set the glass on the oak bar. "Guy came to see me. Said you sent him."

He finished pulling the tie from his shirt. He folded it up and shoved it in his pocket. "Pete?"

"Pluto, yeah."

Mike raised his eyebrows. "He actually came to see you, huh?"

"Yep."

He took a drink from his beer. "I wasn't sure if he was serious or not." He shrugged. "Yeah, I gave him your name."

I looked toward the mass of working stiffs gathering after a day of depositions, day trading, and number crunching. "You know him well?"

He shrugged. "Enough. I handled his mother's estate when she died. Seems like a decent guy."

"You know the brother?"

Mike smirked and rolled his eyes. "Linc? Sort of. He was kind of a little prick the two times he came to my office. I tried to chalk it up to the fact that he'd just lost a family member, but I got the feeling it was a regular thing with him."

As I watched the overpaid yuppies laugh and talk, I thought of Peter Pluto's body in the canyon. Liz hadn't released his name yet, so I didn't feel ready to mention it to Mike.

"What's Peter do for a living?" I asked.

Mike thought about that for a second. "Was selling real estate when I first met him. Assume he's doing it still." He grabbed his glass off the bar. "What's going on, Noah?"

"I'm not sure," I said. "Any idea where the kid would go?"

"No clue," he said. "Pete just said he couldn't find his brother and he was worried. I gave him your name." He paused, stared at me a little harder for a moment. "This have anything to do with the way you look?"

I laughed. "You're not fond of my new appearance?"

"No. It looks like you really pissed off the wrong guy."

I nodded and looked back at the crowd. "Something like that."

"Hey, Noah, if this guy's into something you don't want any part of, don't feel obligated because of me."

I looked back at him. "My curiosity's been piqued."

Mike smiled and drained the rest of his beer. "Fair enough. Well, from what I know, Pete's a good guy. But I really only know him from the estate and trust work I did for him. He was pretty straightforward and completely hassle-free." He set the empty glass back down on the bar. "Like I said, Linc to me was a little bit of a punk. But most of my dealings were with Pete."

"Any way I could find out about that trust left to Linc?" I asked.

He frowned. "Come on. You know that's confidential."

I finished my beer and nodded. "Yeah, but look at my face."

His frown morphed into a reluctant smile. "I don't think there's much there, but I'll see what I can get you."

"Peter said Linc had hooked up with the wrong crowd at some point. Any clue as to what he meant?"

He thought about it, then nodded. "Yeah. Pete tell you anything about the father?"

"He got pretty upset when I asked, so I didn't push it."

Mike nodded, as if that sounded right. "Not surprised. He was into the white supremacy thing. And Linc got into it, too. I'd assume that would be the wrong crowd Pete was talking about."

I thought of Lonnie and Mo. "How involved was Linc?"

"Not really sure," Mike said. "Pete didn't go into it much. I think he was embarrassed by it. I just knew he was worried about him."

"Peter wasn't into it?" I asked.

"I don't think so. Like I said, I don't know Peter all that well. But I highly doubt he's involved with white supremacists. He got visibly upset when he told me that Linc was into it."

It seemed like Linc had been keeping company with a pretty volatile group of friends and I wondered if it had become too much for him to handle.

Mike looked over my shoulder. "And now, if you're finished with me, my date for the evening has arrived."

I laughed and stood. "I said I wouldn't get in the way."

"You are a friend."

"I try."

Mike stood up and waved. "Actually, I think you know her. We were all in court together one time, if memory serves me."

"Really?" I said, and turned around.

The bar was crowded now, people stacked four deep at the railing. The tables in the restaurant were filled completely. Mike could've been waving at anyone in the place, trying to get the attention of any of the gorgeous women in the room.

But it was clear that he was waving at the best-looking woman in the bar.

He was waving at Liz.

She froze for a moment when she spotted me, her expression indicating she was as surprised to see me as I was to see her. But then it was gone and she made her way over to us.

Mike stepped around me. "Liz, you know Noah, right? His eyes were probably different last time you saw him."

She wore a blue blouse and tailored skirt, her hair piled on top of her head. The makeup around her eyes was a little darker than normal, the blue in her eyes a little brighter. She smiled nervously. "Yeah. Hey."

"Hey yourself." I looked at Mike. "I gotta run. I'll call you, alright?"

I didn't wait for an answer. I pushed past them, through the crowd and out the front door, feeling as if I'd taken a beating all over again.

11

I turned up Jonny Lang in the CD player, gripped the steering wheel of the Jeep, and stepped on the accelerator, driving away from the Columbia Street Brewery, Mike, and Liz as fast as I could.

As I forced my way through the traffic headed north on I-5, I unclenched my jaw and tried to relax. Liz and I weren't together. We weren't anything. I didn't have any right to get upset with what she was doing in her personal life, yet my gut felt like it was filled with jagged stones.

I took the I-8 westbound exchange behind the old Sports Arena and past Sea World, exiting at West Mission Bay Drive, and headed into Mission Beach as I thought about my anger. I wasn't ready to admit that Liz was over me. I'd imagined our relationship as one of those like you see on television, where the couple is apart until no one can take it any longer and then they end up back together. You just have that feeling that two people are supposed to be together.

I had that feeling about Liz and me, but she apparently didn't watch the same shows.

I parked the Jeep in the alley outside my house and walked the five blocks up Mission to the SandDune. My legs were stiff and heavy and the walk helped bring them back to life. The bar was half filled; a quiet buzz of conversation mixed with the overhead television monitors.

I slid onto the first stool and waved at Marsha behind the bar. She was wearing a tight black T-shirt cut just above her navel and her blond hair hung straight to her shoulders.

She strolled over and winced. "Who danced on your face?"

"Guy with big feet," I said, leaning against the bar, breathing harder than I would've liked. "Shot of Cuervo and Red Trolley on the back."

She nodded and pulled the bottle of tequila from below the counter. She turned up a shot glass in front of me and filled it with the liquor.

"Gonna be here a while?" she asked, pushing the small glass toward me.

"That's my intent," I said.

She produced a bottle of the beer, flipped the top off, and set it next to the tequila. "Okay. I'll be back in a bit."

I turned my attention to one of the monitors above the bar and watched the Padres play another meaningless game late in the year, trying to shut the image of Liz and Mike out of my thoughts.

It was two beers and an hour later before Marsha wandered back to me.

"You feel as bad as you look?" she asked, throwing her towel into a bin behind the counter.

"Not until people start telling me how bad I look."

She laughed and nodded. "Right. Sorry."

"No problem. I'm getting used to it."

She leaned on the bar. "Guy was in here earlier, looking for you."

I sat up a little straighter. "Really?"

"Yeah. About an hour before you rolled in."

Images of Lonnie and Mo fired through my head. I turned around and did a quick scan of the room. No one with a shaved head.

I turned back to Marsha. "Get a name?"

She shook her head. "Nope."

I could feel the hair on my neck come to attention. "What did he look like?"

"Black guy," she said. "Maybe twenty or so. About your size. Lots of gold on him, wearing a Raiders jersey and a Dodgers cap."

I relaxed a little at her description, realizing it hadn't been Lonnie or Mo. "Say what he wanted?"

"No," she said, pushing herself off the bar. "Came in, asked Marco if he knew you, Marco pointed him in my direction, I told him I hadn't seen you today."

Her description reminded me of Deacon Moreno, the kid that Rolovich had complained about at the apartment complex. If it had been him, I wasn't sure why he'd be looking for me, but I was immediately uncomfortable with the idea that he knew to find me at the SandDune.

I stood up from the stool. "Thanks, Marsha." I fished some money out of my pocket and slid it across the bar. "He comes back, give me a buzz, alright?"

She scooped up the money. "No problem."

I walked out of the SandDune into the cool evening air. Mission Boulevard was heavy with traffic, cars crawling at a snail's pace, but no one seeming to mind. The late summer tourists walked slowly down the street, pointing and smiling at nothing in particular.

A Toyota Camry with a thumping bass coming from the interior broke out of the line of traffic and pulled to the curb in front of me.

I stepped back and reached around my waist, touching the butt of my gun for reassurance.

The passenger window dropped and the volume of the music went down with it. A kid, about eighteen, with skin the color of black licorice leaned out. He didn't match the photo Rolovich had shown me.

"Yo," he said, exposing a gold tooth in the middle of his mouth. "How we get to Garnet?"

I tried to glance around him, but couldn't see the other face behind the wheel. "About two miles up to the north. Same direction you're going."

He leaned on the window, a thick chain around his neck jangling against the inside of the door. "This way? You sure, dude?"

"Yeah."

His tongue snaked out the corner of his mouth and he nodded slowly. "Cool." He lifted his chin as a way of saying thanks, then leaned back in the car. He turned to the driver, said something, and then turned back to me. "Good thing we found you standing out here. Makes things easy, know what I'm saying?" He winked and the window and the volume of the music both went up.

The wink didn't fit as I watched the Camry pull away from the curb, back into the northbound traffic, my heart beating faster than I would've liked. I took a step forward, trying to get an eye on the receding license plate, when I saw the red Escalade coming on the southbound side of Mission.

The back window on the driver's side slid down and two gun barrels poked their heads out like a pair of twin cobras.

The kid in the Camry had done his job and served me up on a platter.

I dropped to the sidewalk, my already aching body taking another jolt, and hit the concrete, the first wave of bullets whistling above my head. Tires squealed, people screamed, and glass shattered as the guns fired into the front window of the SandDune. I ignored the throbbing in my ribs and rolled to the curb, trying to avoid the falling glass and taking cover next to the parked cars on the street.

The gunshots stopped as quickly as they'd started. An engine roared and as I moved to my knees and drew my gun, the Escalade tore down the middle of Mission and jerked left onto Mission Bay at the roller coaster, disappearing around the corner.

It was quiet for a moment and then a cacophony of confusion and fearful voices filled the air.

I looked in through the entrance of the SandDune.

People were starting to stand back up inside, eyes wide with terror and shock. I couldn't tell for sure, but it didn't look like anyone was hurt. Marsha was on the phone, probably calling the police.

I stood up awkwardly, my muscles screaming in pain and my gun hanging impotently in my right hand. I stepped back onto the sidewalk, pieces of the painted glass that had spelled out the bar's name crunching beneath my shoes. Sirens wailed in the distance.

I took a deep breath.

I didn't know where Linc Pluto was.

I didn't know who shot Rachel outside her apartment.

I didn't know why Lonnie and Mo had killed Peter Pluto.

And I didn't know who had just tracked me down in my own neighborhood and tried to ventilate my body with bullets.

But as I stood there amid the gunsmoke, burnt rubber, and chaos, with my stomach in knots and my thoughts speeding through my brain on a conveyor belt, I did know one thing.

It was time to go on the offensive.

12

I spent an hour answering questions for a group of SDPD officers as they tried to clean up the chaos on Mission. I said I didn't know if the shots were aimed at me. That was the truth. I assumed they were meant for me, but I didn't know that for certain and I didn't plan on spending the whole night explaining myself.

Being shot at made me think about Rachel and I hadn't been to the hospital yet to visit her. While I wasn't enamored with visiting a hospital again so soon after being released, I wanted to get out of Mission Beach and I needed to talk to her.

I made the drive to Sharp, my muscles stiffening up and throbbing after another long drive, reminding me that I wasn't recovered yet. I needed one more good night's sleep, but I wasn't sure if I'd get it.

I called the hospital on my way over, asked for Rachel's room. She sounded tired when she answered, but told me she wouldn't mind if I stopped by and gave me her room number.

A lady at the information desk in the lobby directed me to the fifth floor and I found Rachel in her room, propped up in her bed, watching TV.

She looked at me when I stuck my head in the doorway. "Hi."

I held up a hand and waved. The color was gone from her face. Her red hair was pulled back into a sloppy ponytail. She looked small and weak.

"How are you?" I asked.

"I'm okay, I guess."

I pointed at the chair next to the bed. "You mind?"

"No. Go ahead." She watched me sit down. "What happened to you?"

"Got in a fight with the wrong guys," I said, trying to find a comfortable position where my back didn't feel like it was on fire.

"Have you found Linc?"

"No. Not yet."

She turned back to the TV. It was tuned to one of those home decorating shows that I tried to never watch.

"So," I said. "You're going to be okay?"

She hesitated, then nodded. "Yeah."

"Where did the bullet hit you?"

She winced when I said bullet. "Just below my collarbone, I guess. They said it went out my back."

"That's good."

"Unfortunately, it hit my collarbone," she said. "It's fractured."

That was going to make her uncomfortable for a while. "How long will you be here?"

"A couple more days," she said. "They wanna make sure there's no infection and that it starts to heal okay."

"I'm sure it will."

She glanced at me. "Yeah."

We listened to the host of the show ramble on about colors.

"What happened at your apartment, Rachel?" I asked.

"I already told the police."

"I know, and I'm sorry to bring it up again. But can you tell me, too?"

She sighed, kept her eyes on the show. "Someone knocked on the door. We thought maybe it was you again. I opened the door, but no one was there. I walked outside to see if anyone was around. I didn't see anyone, so I guessed someone was just messing with us." She went silent for a moment. "That's when it happened."

"Did you see the gun?"

She shook her head.

"Any cars you recognized?"

She shook her head again. "There were a bunch of cars on the street. I heard this big bang. Then I felt something hit me—hard. After that I don't remember a whole lot other than being in pain." She looked away—I could tell it wasn't easy for her to talk about what had happened. She was still scared and still confused. And she had a right to be.

"I told you I got in a fight," I said. "It was with some

other guys looking for Linc—skinheads, Rachel. Do you know anything about them? Or have you seen them around the apartments?"

She wiped the tears off of her face and took a deep breath. "Skinheads? No. That doesn't sound like Linc." She sighed and turned back to the TV. "Does Linc have something to do with what happened to me?"

"Honestly, I don't know." I started to feel guilty for coming. Her eyes were heavy with fatigue and I wasn't helping. "Can I get you anything, Rachel?"

She sighed again and her eyes fluttered. "Um . . . some more water, maybe?" She turned to the side. "There's a pitcher, but it's empty."

I grabbed the pitcher off the table and stood. "Be right back."

I walked down to the nurses' station and had them refill the pitcher with water and ice. When I walked back into the room, Rachel was asleep.

I set the pitcher back on the table, found the remote and switched off the television, and moved quietly out of the room, letting Rachel get the rest she needed.

After getting back from the hospital and a night of thinking more than sleeping, I woke to find Carter drying himself off out on the patio in the sunshine, his board on the concrete next to him.

He shook his head and water sprayed from his hair like from a Labrador's coat. His wet trunks dripped the ocean all over the ground.

He plopped down into one of the chairs. "I'm getting old."

"Why's that?"

"Little fourteen-year-old kid just put on a demo out there," he said, motioning to the water. "Snapped the board like it was glued to his feet. Just ripped the ocean a new one. I looked like a robot out there compared to the little shit."

I leaned against the doorjamb. "Maybe I can help you recapture your youth."

He ran his hand over his face. "How's that?"

"Do some things that might get us in trouble."

His mood brightened. "Gimme five minutes."

Ten minutes later we were headed east on I-8 to the college area and Linc Pluto's apartment complex.

I told him about the shooting on Mission, but didn't mention anything about seeing Mike and Liz. I had other things to worry about.

"For sure they were aiming for you?" he asked, twisting in the passenger seat of my Jeep and adjusting the seat belt around his large frame.

"Seemed like it. I was the only one standing there."

"The Camry is pretty standard stuff."

"What do you mean?"

He straightened up in the seat. "The young bangers do the setup while the older guys make the hit. Kid probably moved up a rung by getting you to stand still for the hitter."

I nodded, thinking he was right. Even if I had pegged the Camry immediately, about the only thing I could've done was scamper back into the bar, making me an even easier target if they'd chosen to come in.

I took the southbound exchange to 805. "Really bothers me that they knew where to find me."

Carter shrugged his big shoulders. "Yeah, but come on. People know you down there. They know you're a PI. Hell, you use that bar as much for an office as you do anything else."

"Still. Bunch of gang members stick out in South Mission. Anybody that knows me would've known they weren't looking to hire me."

Carter nodded. "Probably. Bigger question, though, Noah, is why."

"Why what?"

"Why does some gang have you on their radar?"

I'd been bouncing the same question around in my head and hadn't arrived at an answer. The only connecting line I could draw to that was Linc's possible relationship with Deacon Moreno. I wasn't sure how I fit into that equation and the connection seemed shaky at best.

As we pulled into Linc's apartment complex, I hoped that something there might be able to offer some answers.

The crime tape was gone from the front of Rachel and Dana's apartment and the complex looked as quiet as when I'd arrived the first time.

Carter leaned forward in his seat. "Jesus. What a dump."

"Pretty much."

"Kid lives here, there wasn't much in his trust fund."

"Or it was a convenient place to hide."

Carter turned to me. "From what?"

I opened the door to get out. "Let's see if we can find out."

I glanced around the parking lot and street, looking for anything out of place. I kept expecting to see Lonnie and Mo show up somewhere and I didn't want to be surprised.

Carter came up next to me. "What are you looking for?"

"Nothing," I said. "Come on."

We walked to Linc Pluto's door.

"You got a key?" Carter asked.

"No," I said. "That's why I brought you."

I knocked on the door and got no response.

I looked at Carter. "All yours."

He grinned and motioned for me to step aside. I did, and he took a couple of steps back from the door. Then he stepped forward, lifted his right leg, and jammed his foot into the door near the lock. The door snapped open and slammed against the wall inside.

Carter swept his arm toward the door. "Right this way."

I looked at him. "I meant that I wanted you to pick the lock."

"Oh." He shrugged. "Shoulda been more specific."

I shook my head and went into the apartment. Carter followed. I inspected the door and saw that the lock was still in place. Carter's big foot had just splintered the wood in the frame. I shut the door behind us and it closed like nothing had happened.

The apartment was as neat and clean as Rachel and Dana's was messy and dirty. An expensive-looking leather sofa rested against the longest wall, a square glass table in front of it with several magazines stacked in the middle. A flat-screen TV hung on the wall across from the sofa and several audio and video components were lined up beneath it. Large photographs of the ocean hung in dark wood frames. A computer hutch with an office chair stood in the corner near the kitchen.

Noticeably absent was the presence of any photos of people. It all looked nice, but it felt empty and lonely to me.

"Place is nicer than yours," Carter observed.

"I don't have a trust fund."

"Guy doesn't live in a shitty complex like this when he's clearly got the means to move somewhere else unless he's got a reason."

"Yep," I said, thinking the same thing. "Check the bedroom. I'm gonna look at the computer."

"What am I looking for?" Carter said, walking toward the hall.

"Big black things that shoot bullets. They're called guns."

"My specialty."

I sat down at the chair in front of the hutch, saw the lights on the monitor and CPU that indicated the computer was dormant, and jiggled the mouse.

"Christ," Carter hollered from the bedroom.

"What?"

"Kid's got, like, twelve-hundred-count sheets. Softer than a monkey's ass."

"Familiar with the texture of a monkey's ass, are you?"

"No. But these are awesome."

Carter was easily distracted.

"Keep looking," I said.

The computer's main screen came up. I looked through the files on the desktop but didn't find anything other than what looked like school homework.

I found the directory and checked the Internet history. Nothing out of the ordinary—a few porn addresses, some sports Web sites, the SDSU address, and a couple of news sites.

Until I got to the last one.

The line read *www.whiteisright.com.*

The phrase immediately brought goose bumps to the backs of my arms. It was like I was looking right at Mo's big forehead again.

I found an AOL icon on his desktop and clicked on it. The main menu came up and I logged on as a guest. After entering my password, the computer connected and I typed *www.whiteisright.com* into the search bar.

"Jackpot," Carter yelled from the other room.

I watched the screen continue to load. "What'd you get?"

"Come see for yourself."

"Hang on a sec."

A very real image of a burning cross flashed onto the screen. The image dissolved into a smiling black man's face. A gun emerged near the man's ear and two cartoon bullets moved toward the side of his head. The bullets hit the face and the smile disappeared from the man's face. The image faded away.

WHITE IS RIGHT!!! flashed on the screen.

My stomach tightened from both the image and my decidedly unpleasant memory of the phrase.

A menu bar loaded on the screen, offering tabs for history, donations, and to find out more.

"Shit, Noah," Carter yelled again from the bedroom. "You gotta see all this."

It wouldn't be hard to remember the address. I

closed down the Internet connection, shut off the computer, and walked into the bedroom.

Carter was sitting at the foot of a queen-sized bed in the middle of the room.

He pointed at the oak dresser next to the closet. "Take a look in there."

The top drawer was pulled halfway out.

It was filled with AK-47s and handguns, probably a dozen total.

"All the drawers, dude," Carter said. "Same shit."

I opened the next one down and found sawed-off shotguns. The three remaining drawers were filled with semiautomatics and boxes of ammunition.

"Kid likes his toys," Carter said.

"Apparently."

"Guy doesn't have that much metal unless he's selling. Or holding."

I nodded in agreement. This wasn't somebody taking an interest in guns or owning a few for protection. An arsenal like this could bring in some serious cash.

Carter stood up and walked over to stand next to me at the dresser.

"Look at this shit, Noah," he said, rummaging through the open drawers, admiring the collection. "Half of these you can't even get on the street. You'd have to go to Mexico or Central America to get your hands on them."

"We know the kid's tied to both a gang and the Nazi boys," I said. "Gotta be the middleman, right?" I nodded at the dresser. "Why else does a college kid build up an armory in his bedroom?"

"Maybe he's afraid of something," Carter said, still perusing the drawers. "Or maybe he's got something that doesn't belong to him."

"Like?"

"Well, nothing goes with guns as good as money does."

"But why?" I said, still not sure. "What the hell was this kid into?"

He shrugged.

"I can tell you," a voice said from behind us.

Carter and I froze and then turned slowly around.

Dana stood in the doorway, the dreadlocks on her head sticking out in awkward angles, the gun in her hands pointed squarely in our direction.

14

Dana motioned for both of us to sit on the bed. She wore a tight camouflage tank top and cargo pants cut off at the knees. The small silver rings were still in her eyebrow and lower lip. With the gun, she looked like some sort of Rastafarian commando.

"I thought you were an investigator," she said, looking at me, her green eyes flashing.

"I am."

"Investigators don't break and enter."

I nodded at Carter. "He did that."

Carter smiled at her. "I like to show off how strong I am."

She looked him over the way she had checked me out the first time she met me. She nodded approvingly. "You do have muscles."

"And in all the right places," he said, the smile getting bigger.

"That remains to be seen," she said. She looked at me. "So why are you back?"

"Because I haven't found Linc."

"Did you think he was in the dresser?" She focused on my face a little harder. "And who knocked the shit out of you?"

I took a deep breath, tired of the questions about my appearance. "Dana, look. I have no idea what's going on with Linc. I know he's not here and your roommate ended up in the hospital. I'm just trying to piece all of this together."

The corners of her mouth twitched down and she shifted her gaze to Carter, then back to me. "Do you know anything about what happened to Rachel?"

I shook my head. "No. I don't know if it's all tied together or what. Like I said, I'm just trying to unscramble all of it."

Her shoulders lost some of their carriage. "I went to see Rachel yesterday. She looks terrible."

I remembered sitting with Rachel and couldn't disagree.

Dana's arms dropped to her sides. She glanced down at the gun in her hand, as if she'd forgotten she was holding it. She tossed it toward me, but Carter reached out and snatched it in midair.

"It's not loaded," she said, sinking down to the floor and resting her back against the wall. "I think it goes in the top drawer."

"You got it from Linc?" I asked.

"Yeah. Gave it to me about a month ago."

"Why?"

She shrugged and pulled on one of her dreads. "Not sure. He came over and said we might want to keep it. Just in case."

"In case of what?" Carter asked.

"He said the people he was working with could be a little freaky and if they ever came to bother us, I could flash it at them and scare them away."

"People he was working with," I said. "Who exactly were they?"

"Don't know." She shook her head. "He constantly had people in here, though."

"Gangs?"

She nodded. "A lot of those guys. I think it started because one of them used to live here."

"Deacon Moreno?"

She looked surprised. "Yeah. Linc started hooking up with him and it just grew."

"What grew?" I asked.

"Whatever he was doing," she said. "I think he was buying and selling the guns."

"You know that for sure?"

"I heard bits and pieces," Dana said. "Pretty sure that's what was going on."

"Where was he getting the guns?" Carter asked.

"No clue."

"Did Rachel know about the guns?" I asked.

Her face sagged a little at the mention of her friend. "Well, yeah. I mean, everyone kind of knew. It was hard not to know. But it's not like any of us talked about it. But because she and Linc were . . . whatever . . . yeah, she knew what was going on."

"Did she have any part in it?"

Dana tugged harder on the dreads. "No. No way. I love Rachel, but she's totally naïve, you know?"

"Did you have any part in it?" Carter asked, turning the gun over in his hands.

She leveled her eyes at him. "No. I knew what was going on. That was it. Got it?"

Carter smiled. "Got it."

I tried to imagine my neighbors in college trading guns as some sort of part-time job, but I couldn't make it work.

"Dana," I said, thinking about what Mike Berkley had told me. "You ever see any skinheads come in here?"

She thought about it, then shook her head slowly. "Not that I can remember. Mostly gang guys, some white drug-dealer kids. That's about it."

Carter looked at me. "So if the guns were here and the bangers were here . . ."

"Then the bangers were buying and the skinheads were supplying," I said, finishing his thought.

"And none of this tells us where old Linc might be," Carter said.

"You have any ideas?" I asked Dana.

"No," she said. "It's like he vanished."

"He ever have money trouble?" I asked, looking around the room.

"No," Dana said, pushing off the floor and standing

up. "He always seemed fine. I guessed it was from the guns."

"Did you ever meet his brother?" I asked.

Her eyes widened slightly. "Didn't even know he had one."

I looked at Carter. "The more I look, the less I find."

"You are wicked good at this detective stuff." Carter shrugged as he handed me the gun. "Guy doesn't wanna be found." He paused for a moment. "And if your client is no longer looking for him, then maybe it's time to give it a rest."

I knew he was referring to Peter's death. Everything was simple arithmetic for Carter. Two plus two equaled four. If Peter was dead, he couldn't pay me. Why waste my time? Carter wasn't completely wrong, but I wasn't ready to let go just yet. Like it or not, I was now involved. Lonnie and Mo had seen to that. Dumping the case wasn't going to remove me from whatever I'd stepped into.

And it wouldn't keep me from looking over my shoulder for my skinhead friends.

I placed the gun back in the top drawer and closed the dresser.

"Did you tell the police about any of this, Dana?" I asked.

She hesitated, the tip of her tongue tickling the ring in her lip for a moment. "I didn't. They didn't ask about Linc. And if they had, I still probably wouldn't have said anything. I don't wanna rat him out."

Her logic was misplaced, but right on for a young college kid.

"You know anyone that bought a gun from Linc?" I asked Dana.

She was staring at Carter and he was staring back. Two people a little off-kilter, caught in each other's tractor beam. I snapped my fingers between them and got her attention.

She looked at me. "There's this one kid. He's in a class with me. I saw him walk out of here with a package two weeks ago, I think."

"Know where he lives?"

"No, but the class I have with him starts in five minutes. I'm bailing today but you could talk to him there."

It wasn't the kind of forward progress I was looking for, but it would have to do for now. There were still more loose ends than I cared to think about, but at least it felt like I was doing something.

Dana moved her gaze from me back to Carter. "You know what?"

Carter smiled. "What?"

A reluctant grin curved her lips. "I'm glad that you're here. You make me feel safe."

"It's my muscles."

I looked at both of them, thought about telling them to knock it off, and then realized what a futile effort that would be.

"Come on, kids," I said, walking between them and out of the room. "Let's go to school."

15

The San Diego State campus is a myriad of gray concrete buildings and asphalt. The administration, in trying to upgrade, courted a major cable company to build an on-campus arena for sporting events, hoping that it might serve as a focal point for the students and foster a new sense of school spirit.

So far, it had led to nothing more than a bunch of empty seats and tuition hikes.

Claphorn Hall was just to the west of the arena and that's where Dana took us to meet her classmate.

"We can wait here," she said, pointing at a stone bench adjacent to the building. "They should be out pretty soon."

"If he went to class," Carter said, taking a seat on the bench.

Dana stood in front of him, pulling her dreadlocks back into a fat ponytail. "He's one of those pretty-boy fraternity types. Trust me. He doesn't miss too many."

"Unlike yourself."

She smiled at him. "Some of us don't need class all the time."

"That happens to be Carter's motto," I said, easing myself down next to him.

"Oh, I've got class," he said, stretching out his long legs, crossing them at the ankles. "I'm just selective about when I show it."

I looked at Dana. "Once in a lifetime would be my guess."

She placed her hands on her hips. "Are you always so selective about showing everything?"

Carter pointed a finger at her. "Depends on what I'm showing. Got something in mind?"

Her smile widened. "I'll let you know."

I shook my head at both of them.

The doors to the building opened and a steady flow of students streamed out into the afternoon sunlight.

"That's him," Dana said, nodding at the last guy out of the building. "I'll go get him."

She headed toward him before I could suggest otherwise.

"I think I'm in love," Carter said.

"I think I'm gonna be ill," I said.

"I think she and I were meant for one another," he said.

"I think she's more than a decade younger than you."

"People say I seem younger than my age."

"They mean you're immature."

"Still."

Dana came back to us, the guy on her heels.

"Guys, this is Donnie," she said, stepping to the side. "Donnie, these are the guys. The good-looking one behind the bruises is Noah and the white-hot-looking one is Carter."

Carter turned to me. "White-hot."

I ignored him.

Donnie was about five-ten, a little on the thin side. A raggedy mop of brown hair sat on his head. A red T-shirt said AZTECS across the chest and his white shorts were fraying at the bottom. The well-worn black flip-flops were almost too small for his feet. One of those biker messenger bags was flung over his shoulder.

"Dana says you guys are looking for a DJ?" he said, his voice higher than I expected.

I shook my head. "Not exactly."

He looked at Dana, then back to me. "Then what?"

"We're looking for the gun you bought from Linc Pluto."

His cheeks flushed and his eyes darted in several different directions. "What? I mean, dude, I don't know what you mean."

Donnie was a bad liar.

"You bought a gun from Linc," I said.

"No. No, I didn't. Who told you that?" he said, shifting his weight from one leg to the other.

"I did, dumbass," Dana said, clearly annoyed at his lack of bravado. "They're not cops. Relax."

He turned to her, the corners of his mouth pinched. "Really? You told me they needed a DJ for some party. So fuck you if I don't believe you, okay?"

Carter sat up a little on the bench. "Easy, there, Backstreet Boy."

Donnie looked at Carter, unsure of how to take him.

"Look," I said. "She's right—we're not cops. I'm a private investigator. I know Linc was selling guns and that you bought one from him. I'm not looking to bust you. I just have some questions I need answers to."

Donnie threw his chest out, adjusting the knapsack. "If you're not cops, I don't have to talk to you."

I nodded. "True."

Donnie tilted his chin upward slightly. "So why don't you and Donkey Kong just fuck off?"

"Because then we'll have to follow you until we get you alone," Carter said. "Then we'll take turns kicking you in the nuts until you feel like talking to us."

I nodded again. "Your choice, man."

Donnie's shoulders slumped, his confidence gone as quickly as it had arrived. "Whatever. What do you wanna know?"

"What kind of gun was it?" I asked.

"A handgun. A thirty-eight, I think."

"You think?"

His cheeks flushed again. "I don't know much about guns."

"Then why did you need one?" Carter asked.

"Because." He took a deep breath, expelling everything in his body, like a child both disappointed and relieved to be caught in a lie. "We sell X out of our apartment."

"We?" I asked.

"Me and my roommates. We're in the same frat. Pi

Kappa Alpha. We're Pikes." He looked at us like that should mean something.

Carter looked at me. "Weren't you in I Phelta Thigh?"

Dana chuckled.

I ignored Carter and focused on Donnie. "You're selling ecstasy. So why the gun?"

He shrugged the perfect shrug of the disaffected youth. "I dunno. We thought it would be cool to have. Just in case or something. Sometimes we have guys who don't wanna pay or try to screw around with us. We figured flashing the gun might take care of that."

I suppressed the urge to smack this stupid kid in the head. He was going to get shot one of these days if he kept waving a gun around that he didn't know how to use. "Fine. How'd you know to go to Linc?"

Donnie looked uncomfortable. "Look, I don't wanna say."

"Why not?"

"Because I don't."

"These two are gonna kick your ass if you don't tell them," Dana chimed in.

"Yeah, well, fine," he said, trying to look like he meant it. "I'll take that over getting killed."

"Killed?" I said. Now we were getting somewhere.

Donnie screwed his mouth into a tight pucker, looked to his left, then his right, then at me. "My roommate knows a guy. From high school. He runs a gang, alright? In Southeast. And he said if we told anybody how we got the gun, he'd kill us. He sent us to another guy, who gave us Linc's address and said to bring five hundred in cash." He paused, shaking his head. "I went to the apartment, guy opens the door, I hand him the envelope, and he hands me the gun. And that was it. Never met him before and haven't seen him since."

So the gang connection appeared to be real, not just imagined by a paranoid landlord or nosy neighbors.

"I need both guys' names," I said. "I'm not gonna tell them where I got them and I'm not gonna mention the gun you bought from Linc. But I need those names."

"No way, dude," he said. "They'll fucking kill me."

"No, they won't, because they won't know how I found them," I said.

"No."

I stood up. "Cool. Then I'm getting the cops to your place in about ten minutes and I'm gonna let them know they'll find a gun, a bunch of ecstasy, and who knows what else."

Donnie stomped his foot. "Fuck! Dude! Don't you understand that they will kill me?"

"I've already forgotten your name," I said calmly, even though I wanted to shake him. Frat Boy was getting on my nerves. "I don't even need an address. Just names."

He stared at me, a scared college kid trying to be tough, caught in a mistake that now frightened the hell out of him. He probably wouldn't sleep for a week. "Deacon Moreno."

Big surprise. "Which one was he?"

"He's the guy who sent us to Linc."

"And the other guy?" I asked. "The one that runs the gang?"

He readjusted the knapsack. "Wizard Matellion."

"Wizard Matellion," I repeated.

"Yeah." He yanked on the strap of the knapsack. "I'm out." He turned and walked away.

I looked at Dana. "That name ring a bell for you?"

She folded her arms across her chest. "Nope."

I turned to Carter. "You?"

"Never heard of him." He stood up from the bench. "But I know someone who might know him and Moreno."

"Who?"

Carter grinned at Dana, then at me. "Someone who's not nearly as white-hot as I am."

That, evidently, was everyone.

16

The three of us piled back into my Jeep and Carter pointed me in the direction of Hillcrest, one of the older, more diverse neighborhoods in San Diego. Not exactly where I'd expect to find answers to my questions, but I'd learned not to question Carter until it became absolutely necessary.

We worked our way south from SDSU on the side streets.

Dana leaned forward from the backseat. "Does Carter work for you?" she asked me.

"Sort of," I said. "But not really."

"What does that mean?"

"Ask him."

She turned to Carter.

He adjusted the blue mirrored Revos on his face. "It means he's not the boss of me."

"Who is the boss of you?" she asked, a note of mischief in her voice.

"I am my own boss," he said, turning around to talk to her. "And I'm an actor."

"No way," she said. "Get out."

We moved through the old homes in Kensington. "Yeah, dude. Get out. I'll even slow down," I said.

Both of them ignored me.

"What have you been in?" she asked, nearly swooning from the excitement of it all.

"Nothing yet," he said, undeterred. "I'm just getting into the business. I'm gonna play a thug."

"Hard to believe," I said, turning us onto University Avenue.

"Can I come watch?" she asked, leaning forward just a little farther so she could place her hand on his arm. "Visit you on the set?"

His giant smile looked clownlike beneath the sunglasses. "I'll see what I can do."

Dana returned the smile and leaned back.

I nearly gagged. "Where am I going, superstar?"

"Turn right on Fifth. Corvette Diner's on the west side."

I moved the Jeep over into the turn lane. "That's where we're going? The Corvette Diner?"

"Yep."

I shook my head as we passed under the arch that signaled the entrance to the Hillcrest community. A collection of bookstores, coffeehouses, and eccentric storefronts, Hillcrest was San Diego's answer to Greenwich Village. As home prices exploded in the suburbs during the nineties, young urban professionals had sought out Hillcrest's affordable one-story bungalows, infusing the neighborhood with new life and new money. Trendy bars and restaurants popped up and disappeared with regular irregularity.

The one mainstay was the Corvette Diner, a 1950s diner with an actual Corvette suspended from the ceiling. Waitresses wore poodle skirts, neon lights gleamed from the walls, and a working soda fountain ran the length of the restaurant. You could expect at least an hour wait any night of the week near dinnertime.

I parked the Jeep in front of the old hardware store just up the street and the three of us walked the block to the diner.

"I hope we're not going here just because you're hungry," I said.

"And I hope you're not whining just because you're a little girl," he said, opening the door to the restaurant for Dana and me.

Carter guided us over to the long bar at the soda fountain and the three of us slid onto the barstools. Sam Cooke's "You Send Me" was coming from the speakers. Midday, the restaurant was almost full.

The guy working the counter looked over at us. He was about five-nine and reed-thin, with caramel-colored skin and dark brown eyes. A small, compact Afro was tucked under a white paper diamond-shaped hat. He wore white pants and a white shirt with a black bow tie.

When he recognized Carter, his eyes narrowed.

Carter removed his sunglasses and smiled. "Willie J. What's going on?"

Willie's frown intensified. "What the fuck you want?"

"Three cherry Cokes," Carter asked.

Willie stared at him for a moment, then grabbed three glasses and filled them with soda. He slid them in front of us.

He looked at Carter. "That all?"

Carter took a sip from the drink and shook his head. "No."

Willie leaned back against the counter. "How did I guess?"

Dana looked at me. I just shrugged and watched the other two.

"I need a little info," Carter said.

Willie didn't look impressed. "So?"

"So I need it from you."

Willie folded his skinny arms across his skinny chest. "I don't owe you nothin' right now. We square as of last month."

Carter tilted his head to the side. "Come on, Willie. You're gonna need my help again. Right?"

Willie squirmed a little, but tried to hold on to his stance.

"We both know I'm right," Carter said. "Your friends are going to come calling again. You just gonna run?"

I had no idea what they were talking about. But I could tell by Willie's body language, as he uncrossed his arms and the angry frown dissolved to resignation, that Carter had him over a barrel.

"You promise to keep them off me again?" Willie said, lowering his voice.

Carter held up a hand. "You got my word."

A crooked smile emerged on Willie's face. " 'Cause they might be on my ass another time soon."

"And I'll be there to keep them off," Carter assured him.

Willie reached out his fist and Carter met it with his own, sealing their deal.

I didn't want to know.

Willie relaxed. "Alright. What you need?"

Carter looked at me.

"Know a guy named Deacon Moreno?" I asked.

Willie looked at me and then at Dana as if he were just realizing we were there. He looked back at Carter. "They cool?"

"They're with me, aren't they?"

Dana tried to cover up a smile with her hand while I attempted to look somewhat trustworthy.

Willie looked back at me. "I know Moreno."

"What's he into?" I asked.

Willie shrugged his pointy shoulders. "Pretty much whatever he wants."

"Guns?"

"For sure."

"He's in a gang?"

He glanced at Carter, needing a little reassurance before answering me. Carter nodded at him.

"South Bay Niners," Willie said to me. "They run everything south of the bridge."

"The bridge?"

"Coronado, dude. South Bay 'cause that's where they run. Niners 'cause they all rockin' nine-millimeters."

Deacon Moreno was a member of one of the nastier gangs in San Diego.

"How about Wizard Matellion?" I asked. "Know him?"

Willie stood up a little straighter and his jaw tightened. "I ain't talking about Wizard."

"Why not?"

He glared at me. " 'Cause dudes who talk about Wizard die. Straight up."

"No one's gonna know," Carter said.

Willie stared hard at Carter, then shook his head. "Wizard is a bad motherfucker."

"He a South Bay Niner, too?" I asked.

Willie laughed at me like I was retarded. "Wizard fuckin' runs South Bay Niners, Sixth Street Triples, and Hoover Down Killas."

Carter looked at him. "He runs the whole area?"

"Fuckin' A," Willie said. "And I ain't sayin' no more about him." He folded his arms back across his chest.

If Matellion was running the whole show, that meant he was responsible for dozens of murders. It was how they moved up. The more you killed, the more responsibility you got. Fucking fantastic—a case I'd originally thought would be easy had just gone from bad to much, much worse.

"You got an address for Moreno?" I asked.

Willie's face screwed up into a tight ball of anger. "How about if I just drive you right up to his door? Introduce you and shit, let him know I was the one who brought your ass there?"

Carter stood up and looked at Dana and me. "Why don't you guys give us a sec?"

Dana stood. "I'm gonna find the bathroom." She walked toward the back of the restaurant.

"I'll be outside," I said.

As I stepped outside into the overcast afternoon, my cell phone vibrated. I didn't recognize the number on the readout.

I flipped the phone open. "Hello?"

"Noah, it's Liz."

I gripped the phone a little tighter. "Hey."

"Where are you?" she asked.

"Working. Why?"

"I need you to come down to the station."

I took a deep breath and watched the traffic go by on Fifth. "Why?"

She paused for a moment, then said, "I just need you to come down, Noah."

"Is Mike gonna be there?" I said before I could think better of it.

Her irritation was nearly tangible through the phone. "Don't be an ass."

"Who's being an ass?" I said, taking a little enjoyment at her annoyance. "Just wondering if your new boyfriend's gonna be there."

"I'm trying to do you a favor, Noah."

I laughed. "Oh, yeah? How's that?"

She paused again and I half expected her to hang up on me. Part of me wanted her to do just that and part of me wanted to start the conversation all over again.

"Your mother's here," she said. "In lockup."

My throat tightened and goose bumps formed on my forearms. I squeezed the phone so hard I thought it might shatter. I shut my eyes, wishing Liz had said anything other than what she had.

"I'll be right there."

17

I sat in the Jeep, staring at the police station.

I'd told Carter about the phone call and he waved me out of the diner. He and Dana would find their own way home.

He understood.

I didn't want to go in angry, frustrated, and disappointed, but I knew I didn't have that much self-control. I just wanted to corral all three of those emotions before facing my mother for the first time in nearly four years.

I struggled out of the Jeep, cursing the fact that my body was still hurting. All the driving I'd done hadn't helped, either. The traffic on Pacific Coast Highway roared behind me. I walked up the steps to the SDPD building and wondered what excuse I was going to hear.

Liz's office was on the third floor and I found her sitting at her desk, studying a file spread out in front of her.

She looked up. "Hey."

"Hey."

"You got here quick."

I slid into the chair against the wall. "Didn't want to change my mind."

She nodded, then rested her chin in her hand. "One of our guys stopped her on Morena. Car was weaving all over the place. She blew a point-two-one."

I laughed, not meaning it. "That low, huh? She must've been taking it easy today."

"I was down at booking when they brought her in," she said. "I recognized her and had her moved to holding."

"She charged yet?"

Liz shook her head. "No. I waived it. We'll let her sober up and she can go. With you, if you want."

I leaned back in the chair and stared up at the ceiling. "Probably better if she was booked. Maybe, for once, she might get it."

"We can, if that's what you want to do," she said. "But I pulled her record. Three DUIs in last four years and a citation for public intoxication. They can't defer her to a program this time. She's out of freebies." She paused. "We book her, she's gonna stay and I can almost guarantee she's gonna get time at Las Colinas."

I looked back at Liz, a mix of emotions running through me. "Maybe it's time for that."

Liz folded her hands on the desk. "She's still your mom."

"Barely."

"Still. But I'll do whatever you want to do."

I pushed back in my chair and stared at the ceiling again. I wanted her to make sure I never had to see my mother again in a jail cell. I wanted her to erase the years I spent growing up while my mother spent them in bars. And I wanted her to pay back my mother for all the embarrassment heaped on me because of her actions through the years.

But I knew Liz couldn't do any of those things.

I rocked the chair forward again with a clunk. "I'll take her," I said. Duty and obligation had won once again.

Liz stood. "Let's go downstairs, then."

I followed her down the hall to the elevator bank.

"You look a little better," she said. "Your bruises are fading."

"I guess. You confirm on Pluto?" I asked, trying to think of anything but what was waiting for me in the basement of the building.

"Yeah," she responded. "Like you said. We got a match on dentals."

"Cause of death?"

"Blunt trauma to the head," she said. "Probably a bat or something like it."

I hadn't felt lucky at the time, but maybe my pal Lonnie had done me a favor by having Mo use just his fists on me.

"We're trying to track down an aunt in the area," she said. "I'll let you know what we find out."

We stepped into the elevator. She pushed the button marked B, the doors shut, and the elevator glided downward.

"Thanks for doing this," I said.

"I figured you'd want to know she was here."

I looked at Liz. She wore a white oxford open at the neck and dark navy slacks. Her hair was down, behind her shoulders. She was looking back at me and her face looked like she needed some sleep.

"Yeah," I said. "And I'm sorry about on the phone and all. I didn't know why you were calling."

She leaned against her side of the elevator. "Because if you'd known why I was calling, you wouldn't have been an ass?"

I shook my head. "No. I might've been less of an ass, though."

The elevator came to a stop.

"I doubt that," she said as the doors slid open.

"Me, too. Just thought I should say it."

I followed her to a counter where she signed a clipboard and motioned for me to follow. We walked down a narrow hallway and she stopped at the corner where it turned to the right.

"There are four cells," Liz said. "She's in the third one. The others are empty, so you'll have a little privacy."

I nodded, looking down the short hall where my mother waited behind bars.

"You want me to go with you?" Liz asked.

I shook my head. "No. It's okay."

"I'll send someone down in a few minutes to release her and do the paperwork."

"Good idea. If she's in the cell I can't kill her."

She nodded. "Yeah. I figured."

I looked at Liz. "Thanks. Seriously. For calling me and doing this."

Liz glanced down the hallway. "I remember when we were in high school. My junior year, your sophomore, I think. I came over to interview you for the school paper. Something about basketball. But you weren't home yet. I sat out on the patio with her for an hour or so. We just talked. Mostly about you." Liz turned back to me. "I remember thinking she was so cool, that I liked her so much. I had no idea what was really going on."

"No one did," I said.

"You never shared it with anyone."

"I did eventually. With you."

"After like, what? Eight years? When we were in college?"

"I don't know. Probably." I shoved my hands in the pockets of my shorts. "I was already missing a father. I didn't need the world to know it was a double whammy."

She studied me for a moment, chewing on her bottom lip. Then she said, "No one would've thought any differently of you."

I shrugged because I didn't believe her and it wasn't something I was looking to dive back into. I knew that my life was different and that now, as an adult, the reflections of my mother's actions didn't shine as brightly on me. But as a teenager, trying to fit in and project a certain image, I knew that some people had looked at me differently.

And it had hurt.

Liz's stare softened and she gestured down toward the cells. "Go see her."

"Okay."

She hesitated for a moment, started to walk back toward the desk, then stopped. She turned around.

"And call me in the next day or two," she said.

"Yeah. I'll let you know what's going on with her," I said.

She ran a hand through her hair and blinked. "For whatever. Just call me."

She turned and walked back toward the elevator.

I watched her go, wishing I were in a different spot so I could ask her what she meant by that.

But I knew why I was there.

I turned back to the short hall that housed the cells. I forced my feet, heavy with anger and resistance, to move, knowing that the longer I stalled, the harder it would be to see my mother.

It was time to say hello to Carolina Braddock again.

My mother looked the same as she always did.

Long brown hair streaked with blond. Porcelain-pale skin. Hazel eyes with fine wrinkles at the corners. A small, lithe frame. She looked a good ten years younger than her actual age of fifty. Somehow, even after thirty years of bludgeoning her system with vodka and wine, the alcohol hadn't aged her the way it did most drunks.

In a bar or behind bars, Carolina Braddock was beautiful.

I stood outside the cell, hands shoved in my pockets. "Nice place you got here."

She was sitting on the cot and turned in my direction. She looked fatigued, not drunk—a special talent of hers that sometimes helped her mask her inebriation.

A surprised smile formed on her face. "Noah. How are you?"

"Good. I love cruising the jail, looking for old friends and family members."

She laughed softly. "Well, you're lucky I'm here, then."

"So lucky."

She stood up from the cot. She wore a sleeveless yellow blouse and navy walking shorts. She ran her hands down the shorts, smoothing out the wrinkles in the cotton fabric. Another small trick she had perfected over the years. It allowed her to collect herself and attempt to present a sober image before she spoke.

She looked at me. "You look well."

She had to be drunk if she thought I looked well.

"Thanks," I said. "So do you." I gestured at the cell. "Save for the bars, of course."

She nodded. "Not my best feature."

"But a familiar one."

She hesitated for a moment, then nodded again. "Unfortunately, that's true." She tilted her head to the side. "And your tongue is as sharp as ever."

Perhaps her most infuriating talent was to turn my own sarcasm against me. It never seemed to sting her the way I wanted it to and I always felt small when she deflected it.

She walked over to the bars, her sandals clapping against the concrete floor. She rested her hands on the metal door.

"How did you know I was here?" she asked.

"A friend of mine works here," I told her. "She thought she was doing me a favor."

"She?"

She knew Liz from years ago, but I didn't feel like giving her any details.

I shook my head. "None of your business."

She shrugged. "Just checking."

We stood there awkwardly for a few moments, each of us trying to avoid looking at the other. A four-year gap in a family relationship is hard to erase in just a couple of minutes, particularly when the parties weren't sure about wanting the chasm to disappear.

Carolina was the first to break the ice. "Where did you get the bruises on your face?" she asked as she studied me with a little more focus.

"Someone's fists."

"Why?"

I shrugged. "Why not?"

My sarcasm may not have fazed her, but I knew that indifference could sometimes get to her.

She pulled her hands from the bars and folded her arms across her chest. "Are you here to tell me my fate?"

I leaned back against the wall. "They're dropping the charges."

She slid her eyes away from me. "The stop was ridiculous anyway. I never moved out of my lane."

"You blew point-two-one. You were lit. So the stop was good. Carolina."

My sarcasm always failed. My indifference was a long shot. But I knew using her first name would draw a little blood because it reminded her that I didn't think of her as a parent.

"You're my ride home, then?" she said, colder than before.

"Have I ever been anything else?"

"You know better."

"No, actually, I don't," I said. "My most cherished memories are propping you up in the passenger seat after carrying you out of some dive."

"Stop it."

"And then lugging you inside the house, only to have you wake up the next day pretending it all never happened."

"Noah."

I smiled. "I mean, honestly. That accounts for a good part of the early nineties, right?"

Her eyes locked on me for a moment, the faint lines at the corners now defined with tension. Her lips were pursed tightly together, contemplating her response. She knew I was right, yet she'd never admit it. She'd always lived in the moment, preferring to ignore the past, no matter what the consequences or how it had affected me.

She dropped her arms from her chest. "I didn't ask you to come here, Noah. If you don't want to deal with me, then just leave," she said, as if it didn't matter to her. "I'll find my own way."

I knew that was true. As many times as I'd rescued her from a bar or a parking lot, there had been just as many nights when she had managed to get herself home. I'd lie in bed, knowing that sometime in the middle of the night at the oddest hour, a car door would slam outside and the front door would creak open, signaling that she was home and I could look forward to the same scenario the next night. If I left now, she'd figure out some way to get out and get back to her life.

An officer approached from down the hall. He looked at me, uninterested. "She going with you?" he said.

I looked at Carolina, my mother. So much of me wanted to say no, just to say it in front of her face and see if there was any satisfaction in walking away from her. See if it made up for all the anger, guilt, and shame I'd felt for so many years.

But a small part of me simply saw my mother and felt sorry for her once again.

"Yeah," I told the guard. "She's going with me."

19

For two people with big mouths, my mother and I were having an easy time keeping them shut.

Carolina and I rode up I-5 from downtown without speaking, the only noise being Ben Harper's whispering from the speakers of the Jeep. The wedge of silence sat between us like an uninvited passenger.

I took the Sea World Drive exit, went east, then made a left on Morena, heading back into a neighborhood that I always did my best to avoid.

Bay Park is a small community cut into the hills that face west over Mission Bay and out to the Pacific Ocean. The majority of the homes were built in the 1950s, but the views and sprawling decks kept their values in the half-million-dollar range.

Sandwiched between the bottom of the hills and the highway was a small cluster of bungalows. Small lots, drab paint, and no views made it an area that the other residents in Bay Park tried not to claim.

I'd grown up in the bungalows and I didn't want to claim them, either.

My mother lived in the same house two blocks off of Morena that she'd raised me in. The blue paint was still faded, the small lawn was still overgrown, and the garage door that always stuck was still half a foot away from closing.

And I still hated it.

I eased the Jeep next to the curb and shut off the engine.

My mother turned to me. "You're living in Mission Beach, right?"

"Yep."

"Same place?"

I nodded. "Same place that you've never been to."

"You've never invited me."

"You needed an invitation?"

She shrugged. "You usually grimace at the sight of me. I figured it would only be worse if I came to your home."

I stifled a sigh. "My grimace is usually related to your level of intoxication."

She looked away from me, out the passenger window.

I stared at what used to be my home. The front window was off my bedroom. I had climbed through it regularly during high school, not because I was sneaking away, but because I hadn't wanted to see Carolina passed out on the sofa as I left. The window had become my portal to the sane world.

My mother turned back to me. "Do you see Carter these days?"

"Almost every day."

"Is he good?"

"Sometimes, but not usually."

She smiled. "I always liked him."

"That makes you one of the few."

"He was a loyal friend. Everyone needs someone like that looking out for them."

I looked at her. "Most of my friends called those people parents."

Her jaw tightened and she looked down at her lap. She folded her hands together tightly, one of the knuckles cracking. "I suppose. But I meant that I was simply glad that you had such a close friend."

I fought the impulse to feel badly about what I'd said. As a teenager, I'd rarely said what I'd wanted to say to her. I'd been afraid. No matter how absentee, she was the only parent I had. Now, as an adult, I wasn't going to regret whatever came out of my mouth. She could try to make me feel guilty, but I would fight it.

She unbuckled her seat belt. "Do you want to come in?"

I looked at the house again. So many nights I had come home and stood outside, not knowing what I would find inside. A passed-out mother. A strange visitor. Or no one at all.

I didn't have a choice then. I always had to go in.

"No, thanks," I said. "I gotta get moving."

She stared at me for a moment, knowing I was probably lying. But then she nodded quickly. "Okay. Thank you for the ride."

"You're welcome."

She opened the door and stepped out of the Jeep. "And tell your friend thank you, too. For doing whatever she did."

"Yeah. I'll tell her."

She cleared her throat, then hesitated as if she were going to say something. She pinched the bridge of her nose, shook her head slightly, and looked at me. "Okay, then. Goodbye, Noah."

She shut the door and I watched her walk toward the house, stepping carefully on the cracked pavers that split the middle of the lawn.

I could feel it coming and I wanted to smother it, to shove it back down wherever it was coming from. I didn't need it, didn't need to set myself up for the disappointment that I knew would inevitably arrive with any attempt at a relationship with my mother. I didn't want to feel like I needed Carolina Braddock in my life in any capacity.

But I couldn't stop it.

I opened my door and stepped out of the Jeep. "Hey. Mom."

She stopped on the front porch and turned around, a mild look of surprise on her face.

"Saturday night," I said.

She stared at me, puzzled. "Saturday night what?"

My throat tightened and I had to swallow before I spoke. "Come to dinner. At my place."

She looked at me for a moment, as if she thought I might be teasing her, ready to pull back the string when she reached for it. When I said nothing, she nodded.

"Saturday night," she said. "Okay."

I watched her walk inside, the anxiety over our next meeting already churning away in my stomach.

20

I drove back to Mission Beach, my body beginning to wear down at the end of the day. It was becoming a regular thing.

My head was aching, too, but that was from the wear and tear of the emotional ride of the last few days more than anything else. I considered swinging by the SandDune for a drink, but I knew the taste of alcohol would remind me of my mother and the blown-out windows of the bar would remind me of Moreno, Lonnie, and all the other unpleasant characters that had planted themselves in my life.

And the more I thought about Carolina coming to my house for dinner, the more reckless it felt. I'd been caught up in the moment and not thinking clearly. Lonnie and Mo knew where I lived, a fact that was starting to weigh on me more by the day. My home wasn't completely safe for me, much less anyone else.

While waiting for a red light to change, I dialed her

on my cell and got her answering machine. I left a stumbling, vague message about meeting at a restaurant in Mission Beach on Saturday rather than my home. I knew she'd take it the wrong way, but I'd deal with that when I saw her.

I opted to park the Jeep several blocks up from my place. I knew the early evening party traffic would be choking the alleys and I didn't feel like fighting it. I took the opportunity to walk down the boardwalk and collect my thoughts.

The air was still as I strolled up the concrete walk next to the beach, the usual evening breeze sucked up by the lingering heat of the day. The water at the edge of the sand rippled like a black canvas tarp. The laughter and conversation that floated around me from the evening revelers as the darkness descended felt familiar and comfortable.

I wasn't sure I wanted my mother coming into this familiar and comfortable environment because all I'd ever known from her presence was disruption. I'd grown accustomed to being on my own, to living in my own world, and I didn't want to adjust any of that for someone I would never be able to fully trust.

A group of people on the balcony of a blue stucco two-story let out a cry of appreciation. I looked up. Beer bottles raised in the air, they rocked and swayed to the muted music from inside their place. I shook my head, smiling. Those yells and cries, the constant stereophonic noise that poured out of the houses up and down the boardwalk, those were the things I knew I could count on.

I hopped the low wall onto my patio and watched the dark ocean roll in and out for another minute. I thought about going in and calling Carter, but I was afraid he'd tell me he was with Dana, and that was something I didn't want to know about. I didn't want to think about the Plutos or the gang members, either. For one night, I needed a breather.

That left Liz. She said to call her.

I pictured her face, the half-Hispanic, half-Italian features that had taken hold of me a long time ago and refused to let go. I had my doubts about whether we could coexist, but I knew that every time I saw her, I felt like we should be trying.

Maybe it was time.

I headed for the sliding door. As I reached for it, I froze.

The door was an inch from being closed.

I pulled my gun and listened.

Nothing.

I eased the door open with my left hand, the gun heavy in my right. No lights and the television was off. Definitely not Carter.

I stepped into the living room and looked into the shadows. Nothing broken or disturbed. I could hear my breathing and tried to relax.

Something was wrong, but I couldn't place it.

I moved over to the front door. The dead bolt was intact and I couldn't see any damage around the lock.

I scanned the room again, then moved down the short hallway toward the bedroom, replaying the living room in my head, trying to compare the picture of what I'd just seen to what it normally looked like. Television, coffee table, sofa. They were all there.

Then it hit me.

The longboard.

I turned back to the far corner of the living room. The longboard that always stood in the corner was gone.

The muscles in my back tightened and my index finger flexed around the trigger of the gun.

Then it hit me again.

The longboard.

Literally.

The board came charging out of my bedroom, slamming into me and knocking me onto my back, the gun flying from my hand. I recognized Lonnie sliding across the top of the board, his momentum carrying him over and past me into the dark living room.

I rolled over quickly and grabbed him by the ankle as he tried to scramble to his feet. He jammed a heel into my mouth, but I remembered last time and I wasn't letting go. The pain that had riddled my body in the previous days had transformed itself into adrenaline.

I got to my knees and threw myself forward, landing on him as he tried to get up. I forced him back down to the floor, I slammed his face into the floor, his nose cracking on the hard surface.

He screamed and I grabbed his hair, pulled his head up, and rammed his face into the floor again, the adrenaline ripping through my body. His body shook beneath mine as I pressed all of my weight into him.

A hand yanked at the waist of my shorts while another grabbed my shoulder, tearing me away from Lonnie. The hands picked me up with the ease of a crane and hurtled me across the living room and into the dining room wall. Red and black clouds exploded in my eyes as I hit the wall back first. Lightning rocketed through my back and legs as I slid to the floor. I shook my head and righted myself against the wall, trying to clear my vision.

Mo was helping Lonnie off the floor. They looked as if they hadn't even changed clothes from the last time I'd seen them.

I tried to get up, but my knees buckled and I slid back to the floor.

"Fucking cocksucker," Lonnie said, a hand across his nose, his voice wet and muddled. "You fucking cocksucker."

I tried to rise up again, made it halfway before my knees gave out again and I fell to my left. My hand landed on something steel, something cold, something friendly.

My gun.

I slid the gun next to my leg, my hand locking onto it like a magnet.

"I told you'd we'd be back," Lonnie said, removing his hand from his face and exposing what looked like a smashed piece of clay where his nose should've been. Blood oozed from his nostrils and he'd smeared it across his mouth. "Here we are, asshole. And you're gonna talk this time."

"How about Mo steps outside, you little piece of

shit?" I said, trying to sit up straighter against the wall. "You want me so bad? Let's go. Just me and you. Or does Mo always do your fighting for you?"

"You can't handle me, motherfucker," Lonnie sneered.

"I've done it twice, dumbass," I said, tightening my grip on the gun. "And I'm just wondering. Do you call him Mo because it's short for Mommy?"

"You're fucking dead," Lonnie said, moving toward the glass slider. He reached for the hanging blinds and started to pull them closed. "Grab him, Mo."

Mo grunted and took a step toward me.

"Don't fucking move, Mo," I said, raising the gun and aiming it at his chest.

He looked at it, a blank expression on his face. No fear, no anger. As if I were holding a plate of cookies and he wasn't sure if he was hungry. He turned to Lonnie.

Lonnie, on the other hand, looked a little scared, his hand frozen on the cord to the blinds. He licked the blood on his lips and shook his head slowly. "You think that matters?"

"I'm guessing, yeah, it does," I said, keeping the gun on Mo and glancing at Lonnie. "Seems to have frozen your mommy right in his footsteps. Wanna give him a kiss?"

Lonnie stared at me, his eyes cold and flat, full of hate. He looked at his hand, his red fingertips illuminated by the moonlight from outside. Then he looked back at me, a small, ugly smile emerging on his small, ugly face.

He looked at Mo. "Get him."

Mo turned and rushed at me. I froze for a second, stunned that he would charge me with a gun aimed at his chest just because Lonnie said to.

Then I squeezed the trigger.

The bullet hit him in the right shoulder and he grunted, stopping in midstep, his eyes still locked on me.

Lonnie moved for the glass slider and I jerked the gun in his direction and fired. The slider shattered and Lonnie disappeared into the shower of glass.

I swiveled the gun back at Mo. He had his left arm across his chest, his hand covering the expanding wound. He pulled his hand away and examined the blood like a child cut for the first time.

"Let's go!" Lonnie screamed from outside.

"Don't move," I said, locking the gun on him.

Mo reacted as if he didn't even hear me. He pivoted and I fired, but the shot missed high.

Mo jumped the coffee table and charged through the shattered glass door faster than a man with a bullet in his body should've been able, following Lonnie out into the night.

21

Detective John Wellton said, "A little cold in here last night?"

He was standing where my sliding door should've been, the early morning fog rolling up off the water and trying to work its way into my house. Wellton wore black jeans and a white golf shirt, his ebony skin even darker against the shirt. His gun was holstered at his waist. He had his hands on his hips, his legs slightly spread, and I wondered if he thought that stance made him look taller.

"Yeah," I said, standing in the middle of the living room. "So be careful."

"Careful?"

"I don't want anyone mistaking you for a penguin."

He rolled his eyes. "No wonder people want to beat your ass."

"And here I thought it was because they're jealous of my good looks," I said. "What do you want?"

"I was on my way to work. I called the station to check the overnight action. Recognized your address." He looked around the room. "Thought I'd come over and check it out for myself."

"They didn't wake your ass up in the middle of the night?" I said.

He shook his head. "Shit, no. They only do that for the fun stuff." He grinned. "Now, if they'd killed you, I for sure would've been here."

The police had arrived within minutes of Mo's dash out my door. Someone had heard the gunshots and dialed 911. I explained what happened to the cops, told them to check with Liz or Wellton, and then they left. I'd spent the rest of the night taking aspirin for the aches and pains that had taken on a new vigor, sweeping up glass, and glancing at my patio, wondering if I could get to Mo and Lonnie before they decided to return.

"Same two guys that put you in the canyon?" he asked, leaning against the doorframe.

"Yep. They were here when I got home."

"And you shot one of them?"

"The big one. Mo. Upper right quadrant, not that it did any good. You'd need an elephant gun to bring the guy down."

"And the other one?"

I gestured to where he was standing. "I missed him and bought myself a new slider."

"They didn't have guns?"

"Not that I saw."

"Fits them," he said.

"How?"

His face hardened a little. "Fuckers think they're so tough, they don't need guns. Like to use their boots and fists." He paused. "Makes it up close and personal for them."

Wellton may have been short in stature, but the look on his face would've scared off giants.

"At least you look better than the last time you ran into them," he said after a moment.

I nodded. I'd been on edge ever since I'd woken up in the hospital, knowing they'd eventually show their faces.

"I was ready," I said.

"So you were," he said. "Can't imagine a guy bleeding from the shoulder with a tattoo on his forehead will be hard to find, but don't count on it."

"I won't," I said. "You get anything yet on the shooting at the apartment?"

He frowned and folded his arms across his chest. "Nothing. Parents came in, didn't seem to know much. We're still checking with some of the others at the complex and trying to follow up with some supposed friends. There were a couple of drive-bys in the same area last two days." He shrugged. "Could have been just bad timing on her part to step out of her place when she did."

The image of Rachel collapsing to the ground flashed in my head. Too many other things pointed to it not being random.

"I got one other thing for you," he said. "We got in touch with Peter Pluto's aunt. She's coming in at noon to do some paperwork. Liz thought you might want to talk to her."

I shifted gingerly on the sofa, my back stiff. "And Liz couldn't tell me that herself?"

Wellton laughed and glanced over his shoulder toward the beach. "Don't worry. She won't be there. You won't have to use your indifferent bullshit act you like to put on when she's around."

It irritated me that Wellton could decipher what was going on between Liz and me. I had a hard time believing that she would share our relationship with him, but he was her partner and partners talked.

"So why's she got you running her errands?" I asked.

"Probably for the same reason you just shit your pants when you thought you were gonna have to face her this afternoon," he said. "You're both too chicken to deal with each other."

I felt the blood rush to my face.

"Hey, man," he said. "She's doing you a favor, alright? It was me, I'd say fuck it and leave you out of it because you bring trouble like a skunk brings stink." He frowned. "But she said to tell you, so I'm telling you. Come down or don't come down. I could give a shit."

I wondered if he was right about Liz's reason for avoiding me. I thought some of the awkwardness had disappeared between us when I saw her at the station, but he was right, at least on my account—I still hadn't worked up the courage to tell her exactly how I felt about her.

I pushed myself up. "Alright. I'll be there."

"Fantabulous," he said. "Can't fuckin' wait."

"This is really on your way to work?"

He nodded. "I live in Pacific Beach, off of Lamont."

"Really?"

"Despite whatever cultural myth you subscribe to, black guys like the beach, too," he said. "I just tell everyone I tan real good."

I laughed. "Sure. Well, seriously. Thanks for coming by. I appreciate it."

He looked at me warily. "Yeah. You're welcome."

"And thanks for not bringing the other six dwarves or Snow White with you," I said. "Woulda been weird."

He shook his head, showed me his middle finger, and left.

The glass man showed up at nine on the dot to hang my new patio door. I showered while he worked, letting the hot water take some of the sting out of my banged-up body. An hour later the door was in and the evidence of my poor aim with a gun was gone.

I grabbed a breakfast burrito at Roberto's and, with time to kill before meeting the Pluto aunt at noon, I headed back up to Linc's apartment to see if anything or anyone showed up.

I parked just down the block and sat there with my breakfast. Some cars came and went. Dana headed out with a backpack full of books and climbed into a Nissan Xterra by herself, apparently on her way to class. Rolovich came out for a smoke.

Other than that nothing much happened, so at eleven-thirty I headed downtown to meet Peter and Linc's aunt. I'd known it was a long shot that Linc would just happen to walk by while I was sitting there, but there you go—I'm a dreamer.

The morning fog was still hanging around, covering I-5 like a tunnel, and the traffic was thick going south. We moved along slowly, but my normal impatience didn't rear its head. Something about defending myself in my own home had relaxed me, made me more confident. I held my own against Lonnie and Mo and came out on the better end.

I found a parking spot two blocks up from SDPD headquarters five minutes before noon, dropped change in the meter, and headed over to the big building.

Wellton was standing in the downstairs lobby. A woman was with him.

"Hey," I said as I approached.

"Hey," Wellton said. He gestured at the woman next to him. "This is Marie Pluto. Ms. Pluto, this is Noah Braddock."

Marie Pluto stood about five-seven and looked to be in her late forties. Dark hair fell to her shoulders, her face bearing the strain of someone who has just lost a relative. Sad gray eyes surrounded by fine wrinkles and a small mouth smiled politely at me.

She offered her hand. "Hello."

"Hello," I said. "I'm sorry for your loss."

She looked away for a moment. "Thank you."

"Mr. Braddock is the investigator I was telling you about," Wellton said. "Your nephew hired him before his death."

"To find Linc?" she asked, her focus back on me now.

"Yes."

"Have you found him?"

"Unfortunately, no. But I was hoping I could ask you a few questions about him."

"Certainly. I'll help however I can."

"Ms. Pluto, thank you again for coming by to take care of the paperwork. My condolences," Wellton said. He shook her hand. "I'll let you two speak."

"Thank you, Detective," she said, taking a deep breath.

He turned his attention to me. "Stop by when you're done, alright?"

I knew he would want any info I got from Marie. He set up the meeting, so it was only fair.

"Sure," I said.

We watched Wellton walk down the hallway and disappear around a corner.

"Do you mind if we walk outside?" she asked. "I could use the air."

I nodded and we walked out through the crowded front lobby and into the cool midday air, sitting down on the steps facing Broadway.

"When did Peter hire you?" she asked, folding her hands in her lap.

"Last week," I said, realizing it felt more like a month.

"I assume you know what happened to Peter?"

I thought about seeing him in his house and lying next to him in the canyon. "Yes. I'm sorry."

She took a deep breath and stared at the street. "Peter was a good kid. I mean, he wasn't a kid, but that's how I thought of him."

"You were his aunt?"

She nodded. "His father was my brother. And he wasn't much of a father." She paused. "Peter figured it out early on, but I don't think Linc ever did."

I didn't say anything.

"You know that their mother died?" she said.

"Peter told me she had cancer and died two years ago. He mentioned a small trust fund that Linc was living off of."

Marie nodded. "Her family had a little bit of money and her parents left it to the boys. Nothing to make them rich, but enough for them to be alright." She leaned forward and rested her forearms on her knees. "Their grandparents just wanted to make sure that their father didn't get his hands on it."

A group of Japanese tourists stopped across the street and pointed their cameras at the police building. I couldn't imagine who told them that it was something to photograph. They smiled at one another and moved on.

"Was your brother still in contact with the boys?" I asked.

"Peter shut him out and he stopped trying," she said, looking at me. "But he was still talking with Linc when he was killed."

"Killed?"

"Stabbed in a fight," she said, her voice void of emotion.

"I'm sorry."

She smiled. "Don't be. He probably deserved it."

The Pluto family just kept getting stranger.

We watched the afternoon traffic move by on Broadway for a few moments, the din of the taxis and cars filling the awkward silence. The fog was finally dissipating and the smell of wet concrete drifted in the air.

"If you would, I'd like you to keep looking for Linc," she said. "I'll pay you."

I nodded, that tiny, self-centered devil on my shoulder applauding. "I'd be happy to keep looking."

"Thank you."

It wasn't just about the money for me, though. Being attacked and shot at had given me my own incentive to find Linc and figure out how it all meshed together.

"Anything you can tell me about Linc that might help?" I asked.

She shook her head. "Not that I can think of. He withdrew from pretty much everyone after his mom died. I kept tabs on him through Peter." She paused. "He was going to San Diego State, but I'm assuming you already know that."

I nodded. "I do. I've learned a few things, but I'm not sure how they all fit together."

"Such as?"

"I believe he was selling guns primarily to gang members."

Her eyes widened. "What?"

I told her what I'd found in Linc's apartment and about the connections with Wizard Matellion and Deacon Moreno.

She stared at me like I'd told her that San Diego was in Arizona. "Good Lord."

"And I think he had something to do with a hate group, too," I said. "It looks like he was using his connections to both groups. Selling guns for the skinheads to the gang members."

"Oh, Linc," she said, clearly frustrated by her nephew's actions.

"Can you tell me anything about his involvement with the hate group?"

She was quiet for a moment, gathering her thoughts. "Have you ever heard of National Nation?"

"No."

She shook her head. "My brother, their father, was a member. Very involved. He held some kind of office or something."

She paused, the anger forming on her face.

"We all were disgusted by it," she said, her voice rising a little, gathering steam. "And ashamed. And embarrassed. Peter, of course, knew what it was immediately and wanted no part of it." The lines around her mouth drew tighter. "But Linc didn't. And then Linc decided he kind of liked it."

Marie sighed. "As I said, my brother, Anthony, was some sort of leader in it. It took over his life and he died because of it. Went after some black kid and got stabbed." She shook her head. "I wanted to feel bad about his death, but I couldn't. The world was a better place."

"Linc stayed involved?"

"I'm not sure to what extent," she answered. "But I

know he was still doing things for them. I caught him handing out literature with their slogan on it."

The afternoon sun surfaced in the sky and beat down on my face, my skin tightening against the heat.

"White is right," I said.

She turned to me, surprised. "Yes. That's their slogan. So you have heard of them?"

I had.

I thanked Marie Pluto for her time after we exchanged phone numbers and she wrote me a check to retain my services. I told her I would keep her informed and headed off to find Wellton, my mind buzzing.

Linc had put himself in a horrendously dangerous position. I'd already figured out that he was selling the skinheads' guns to the gang members. I wondered about the extent of his involvement with National Nation, though. I had a hard time believing that someone devoted to purifying the white race would have any dealings with African-Americans, even if there was money involved. Just like everyone else, bigots had their limits.

And above everything else, what would be worth putting yourself in such a dangerous spot?

I found Wellton in his cramped office. I slid into the chair across from him.

"Anything?" he asked, pushing back from the desk.

"No," I said. "But I need to come clean with something."

"Oh, shit," Wellton said, rolling his eyes. "Here we go."

"There are guns in Linc Pluto's apartment," I said, knowing I couldn't keep it from him any longer. "I didn't tell you at first because I didn't think it was related to Rachel's shooting."

" 'Didn't think' is the key phrase there," Wellton said, irritated.

"Whatever. I'm still not sure it's tied to Rachel. But I think they are tied to Linc's disappearing act and Peter's death, not to mention the beating I took."

Wellton gritted his teeth. "Why in the fuck would you not tell me that before?"

"When Peter came to me, he knew Linc was in trouble. He was trying to find his brother and keep him from making a mistake. I was doing as my client asked," I said. "And like I said, I'm still not sure it's relevant to the shooting at the apartments."

"Would've been nice to know there was a room full of guns next door to the vic's apartment," Wellton grumbled.

"Hey. There could be guns on the other side of that apartment, too. You saw the place."

Wellton stared at me. "Are the guns still there?"

"Should be."

Wellton exhaled and it sounded like a hiss. "Dazzle me with why you think the guns are tied to Pluto's death."

I laid out Linc's involvement with both groups and

what Mike Berkley and Marie Pluto told me about his involvement with National Nation.

He tapped his finger on his chin. "I hate to say it, but that makes sense. Of course, if I'd known what you knew when you knew it, I might've put that together, too."

I didn't say anything.

Wellton leaned back in his chair and brought his feet up on his desk. "Okay. Let's say you're right. He's a member of this group and he's dealing guns to the bangers."

"I don't see anything else that fits."

"You think either side knew what he was doing?"

I shook my head. "I don't see how. No way skin-heads would be cool doing business with a black gang, and I'm pretty sure the gang would feel the same way."

"So he was freelancing."

"Have to think so. I just don't get why."

"Pretty dangerous work," Wellton said, rubbing his chin. "And pretty fucking stupid. Either side finds out, he's a corpse in a hurry."

"Maybe one side found out," I said.

"Maybe."

We sat there in silence.

Wellton pulled his feet off the desk. "You gonna keep chasing this kid?"

"I told the aunt I would," I said.

"Plus you got a little score to settle," he said.

"Maybe."

"Maybe my ass." He looked at me. "You know much about hate groups?"

"Not really. Just what I've read."

He grabbed a Rolodex from the corner of his desk and thumbed through it. "Sick fuckers. Poorly organized, but funded enough to keep doing their thing."

"They have big numbers here in San Diego?" I asked.

"Fair amount," he said, flipping through his Rolodex. "Not as much as some cities, but enough to make trouble." He copied something off the card onto a notepad, then stared at the piece of paper. "Can't believe I'm about to ask this."

I stayed silent, not wanting to ruin the moment.

"If you're gonna keep looking, I could use your help." He spoke deliberately, as if he weren't sure of the words. He gestured at a two-foot-high stack of folders on the desk. "I'm buried here. And I got no end in sight. If you wanna share what you get, I'll do the same."

"You want me to get involved?" I asked.

"You already are."

"But I have your permission to poke around and stir things up?"

"Just around this Linc kid," he said, raising an eyebrow. "Share what you find. Like, say, an apartment full of guns. You find shit like that, I wanna know."

"You wanna deputize me, make it official? Maybe we could hug or something?"

"I am not the cure for your jungle fever." He tore the sheet from the pad and handed it to me. "Talk to this guy."

The name Gerald Famazio and a phone number were on the paper. "Who's this?"

"Professor at USD. Sociology, but he specializes in hate groups. He can probably give you a few names, let you know where to find some folks."

I nodded and stood. I folded the slip of paper and dropped it in my pocket. "Liz in her office?"

He grunted. "No clue, loverboy. Go look for yourself." Then he grinned. "Or you want me to give her a note or something? See if she wants to meet you out behind the gym? Then I can come back and tell you and we can huddle together and figure out what to do next." He clapped his hands together. "It'll be fun. All sixth grade and shit."

"When you were in sixth grade, were you big enough to sit in your own desk?" I asked. "Or did you have to sit on someone's lap?"

"Get out," he said, the smile disappearing from his face.

I left and walked down the hall toward Liz's office. I heard voices coming through her doorway, hesitated for a moment, then stepped into the office.

Liz was leaning back in her chair, arms folded across her chest, laughing easily. Her hair was pulled back away from her face. Bright red blouse, silver bracelets on each wrist matching the big silver hoops in her ears.

Across the desk from her, Mike Berkley was laughing, too.

She looked up at me, surprised. "Hey."

Mike turned toward me. He wore an expensive-looking navy suit, light blue collared shirt, and yellow tie. "Noah. What's going on?"

Dumb fucking luck.

"Didn't mean to interrupt," I said, trying to keep the tension that was running up my spine out of my voice.

"You're not," Liz said quickly, shaking her head for emphasis. "Mike was just leaving."

He glanced at his watch and stood up. "I was, in fact. Hey, I read about Peter Pluto in the *Union-Tribune*. Did you find Linc yet?"

"Not yet," I said. "Still working on it."

He shook his head. "I didn't mean to get you involved in this crap. I'm really sorry."

"It's okay."

"I'm having the trust records pulled and some other paperwork put together for you," he said. "Least I can do."

"Great," I said.

"Okay," he said, then faced Liz. "I'll call you later."

"Fine," Liz said, looking down at the desk.

I stepped out of the doorway.

Mike gave me a friendly punch in the arm as he passed. "I'll call you when that stuff's ready."

I thought about punching him back, but was afraid I might knock him off his feet. "Yeah."

I watched him walk down the hall, then stepped back into her office.

"He didn't have to leave," I said.

"Don't," she said, pointing a finger at me. "I don't want to hear it."

I leaned against the doorframe. "I didn't realize when you said to call you, you meant call first so I wouldn't walk in on you two."

"Fuck you, Noah. Seriously. Fuck you." She shook

her head, frowning, then just shrugged. "John told me about last night. Are you alright?"

"I'm fine."

"Did you meet the aunt?"

"I did."

"And?"

"And I shared the conversation with Wellton."

She shifted her eyes away from me, her jaw tightening.

I couldn't help it. I had no real reason to be angry with her. Or Mike, for that matter. But I was, and I didn't care anymore.

Her eyes came back at me. "Why are you here? Did you just stop by to be a dick?"

"No."

She stood up. "Then why the fuck are you being one?"

"I didn't know you two were so serious," I said, ignoring the question.

"Like it's any of your goddamned business what we are."

"I didn't say it was."

"No, but you seem really interested, so let me tell you what you wanna hear," she said. "He's great in bed. Unfuckingbelievable, really."

I shrugged. "Whatever."

"Jesus Christ," she said, her hands coiling into fists at her sides. "Are you nine years old? When do you break out the sticks-and-stones line?"

I felt the blood rush to my face, a mixture of anger and embarrassment.

And jealousy.

"I gotta go," I said, turning to leave.

"No. Wait."

I turned back around to face her.

"You can't keep doing this," she said. "You can't keep getting angry with me over this."

I stood there silently.

"I said to call me because I wanted you to," she said, looking me right in the eye. "I started thinking that maybe I was wrong in bailing out on us last time. But now I'm not so sure. You act one way one minute and another the next. I have no idea what is going on with you and, honestly, it's getting old."

She grabbed a file off her desk and walked toward me. She stopped in the doorway, our faces inches apart. "If you want me back in your life, say it out loud."

I swallowed hard, feeling claustrophobic under her gaze. "I want you back in my life."

"Then quit acting like such an asshole."

She turned and walked out of the office and down the hallway, leaving me to figure out how to do that.

24

I left before I could embarrass myself any further.

Liz's words echoed in my head as I walked to the Jeep. For all the yelling and swearing she'd done, she'd left the door open for something between us. Now I just needed to step through that door without getting it slammed in my face.

I called the number Wellton had given me for Professor Famazio and got a voice-mail message that told me he held daily office hours from two to three in the afternoon. That gave me just enough time to stop at Filipi's on India for a slice of pizza and work my way over to USD.

While San Diego State was large and impersonal, USD was cozy and welcoming. The campus sat atop a bluff looking out over Mission Bay, the Pacific, and Sea World. White stucco Spanish-style buildings dotted the bright green lawns on top of the hill. The center of the Catholic university was the Immaculata, a cavernous church built in the shape of a cross and topped with a pale blue dome. San Diegans referred to the school as Notre Dame West.

The sociology department was located in Founder's Hall just past the Immaculata and I found Professor Famazio's office on the second floor at the end of a long hallway.

The door was closed halfway. I knocked lightly and a voice beckoned me in.

The small office looked larger than it actually was because everything in the room was precisely placed. The books on the pine bookshelves were lined up evenly and the papers on the desk were stacked so that not a single corner stood out. A small window on the far wall showcased a portion of the afternoon sunshine and brightened the already light room even more.

Professor Gerald Famazio sat in an oversized leather chair behind the desk. He was somewhere in his early forties, and the closely cropped black hair on his head was flecked with gray. Wire-rimmed glasses magnified small, intense brown eyes that matched the color of his skin. The navy polo shirt on his athletic frame and brown corduroy jacket hanging on the back of his chair were standard issue in academia.

"Can I help you?" he asked, pushing back a little from the desk, his deep voice filling the room.

"I hope so," I said, handing him my card. "My name's Noah Braddock. I'm an investigator. Detective John Wellton gave me your name."

He glanced at the card, then back at me. "You work for the police department?"

I shook my head. "No. I'm private, but Detective Wellton and I are looking at some things that seem to overlap. He said you might be able to help me."

He eyed me for a moment, not bothering to hide his apprehension. He set my card on his desk, stood, and offered his hand. "Gerald Famazio." We shook hands and he gestured at a wooden straight-backed chair next to the desk. "Have a seat."

I slid into the chair.

"John has been generous to me," he said, lowering himself back into his chair. "Letting me rummage through his files and whatnot, answering numerous questions when I know he had other things to do." He paused for a moment. "So I'll repay the favor if I can."

"I guess I'm mainly looking for a place to start," I said. "With something called National Nation."

A tight smile formed on his lips. "Unfortunately, then, I'm your man."

"That's what he said."

"What do you know about the group?"

I explained to him the basics of my involvement with Linc, Peter, Lonnie, and Mo.

He raised an eyebrow when I finished. "That's surprising."

"Which part?"

"That they let you live." He folded his arms across his chest. "Normally, their assaults result in death."

I thought of Peter Pluto lying in the canyon and how close I had probably been to joining him, but said nothing.

"But maybe you are a novelty for them," he said. "An opponent who can fight back."

"Let's just say I'm on guard."

"A good thing to be with these guys," he said. "Because they aren't rational and they are very persistent."

"I'm starting to get that impression."

He adjusted the glasses on his face. "National Nation is an offshoot of Aryan Nation. They have roots here in San Diego. They became organized and active about ten years ago." Something flashed through his expression and disappeared as quickly as it had appeared. "So they are still young in terms of their history. Are you familiar with White Aryan Resistance?"

I nodded. You didn't grow up in San Diego without having some awareness of the group that had formed in the northern suburb of Fallbrook. A television repairman had started the group in the early eighties and gained some national prominence with his antics. At the time, Fallbrook—a small, rural, almost entirely Caucasian community that wasn't entirely open to change—had been the perfect place for his base.

But as the demographics of the county changed, Fallbrook went from rural outpost to a suburb with million-dollar properties amid the avocado groves. The town was now doing the best they could to distance itself from the racist label.

"This group you're talking about split from them," Famazio said.

"Are they involved in gun trafficking?"

"At some level. But if you're referring to an organized business operation to make money, then no." He shook his head. "They don't have the discipline to put together something of that order. They refuse to commit their time to something that, in a perverse way, would legitimize them."

I could hear something in his voice that he was trying to hide. Disdain or disgust, maybe. I assumed that much of what he saw in his work offended him personally.

"Are they opposed to everything outside of the white race?" I asked.

"Yes and no, and that's what distinguishes them right now," Famazio answered. "They believe that whites are superior and that all other races are inferior. But they believe blacks pose the biggest threat and, as such, work almost exclusively against them."

"You said that they refuse to commit their time to something like guns. So what do they do with their time?"

He adjusted the glasses again and sighed. "Perpetuate violence. If you look at most hate groups, they rarely possess the brain trust to organize into a viable financial operation, which leads to eventual demise." He waved a hand in the air. "They subsist on donations from extreme right-wing groups and anonymous donors who are too cowardly to show their faces and their own money. They stay alive because the powerful white men that help serve justice in our society—judges, lawyers, even police officers—are sometimes believers and help them avoid consequences under the guise of the law."

We let that hang in the air between us.

"Anyway, the opposite end of the spectrum is, say, organized crime or street gangs," Famazio continued. "They've learned that a solid business structure provides them with not only funding for their activities, but also the power to grow and influence."

"So National Nation is content to pass out fliers, graffiti some walls, and beat up black people?"

"Kill," he said, staring at me. "They kill black people."

His anger radiated across the desk.

"National Nation is still in its infancy compared to other groups," he said. "That's why I've had such a difficult time learning names of members and backers for my research. They in no way possess the sophistication, for lack of a better word, of a group like the KKK." He shook his head. "These . . . people . . . like to consume a lot of alcohol, talk about their grand plan for taking over the world, and then go beat some black person to death." He looked away from me. "It's what they do and it's what they enjoy."

I shifted in my seat, uncomfortably aware of the difference in our skin color. "Where would I go to find them?"

He looked back at me. "Two run-ins aren't enough for you?"

"I need to find this kid and I think he might be with them."

"This kid, if he's a member of National Nation, may not be worth finding."

"All due respect, Professor, but that's something I need to find out for myself."

He studied me for a moment and I couldn't tell if he was angry or amused with me.

"John tell you anything about me?" he asked.

"No. Just that you might be able to help me."

"No mention of how he and I met?"

I was missing his point. "No."

"Mind if I show you something, then?"

"No."

He pushed himself out of his chair and came around the desk, the strain on his face unmistakable. The limp was impossible to miss, as the lower part of his right leg from the knee down dragged behind him, seeming heavier and less coordinated than the rest of his body.

He eased himself onto the edge of his desk. "I thought I could take care of myself, too, Mr. Braddock. Knew I was smarter than them and I figured that would make a difference." He pointed to his right leg. "I've got more pins and screws in there than a hardware store. Can't feel my toes. There is an ache in my calf that won't go away and keeps me up most nights."

He removed the glasses from his face. "My leg was shattered in twenty-three places, courtesy of a lead pipe and an aluminum bat. They beat me all over my body and the only reason they didn't kill me was because they thought I died when I passed out. John Wellton worked the case."

He leaned down so that our eyes were on the same level. "So, if you're sure you wanna go meet these fellows, I've got a thank-you card to send with you."

I moved my eyes from his gaze, embarrassed by my own ignorance and furious with Wellton for sending me to Famazio so unprepared. It didn't change what I needed to do, but it did make me look at it in a new light. I wouldn't be going up against just the two guys who'd nearly killed me. I'd be taking on an entire organization that prided itself on violence.

I looked back at him. "I'm sorry."

"Yeah," he said, sitting back upright and placing the glasses back on his face. "Most folks are."

"But you said yourself you're still looking for names. You're still working these guys. What happened to you didn't stop you."

He was the one who looked away this time.

I stood up. "I need to find this kid. If you can't help me, fine. But it's not going to stop me from looking. His brother is dead, another girl almost died, and I think he's tied to both. If I quit now, everybody loses. And that includes me and you."

He turned back to me, started to say something, then stopped. His jaw clenched and he shook his head. He stood up and moved back around the desk. He opened a drawer in the desk and yanked out a small notepad. He scribbled on it, tore the sheet off the pad, and held it out to me.

"A campground," he said. "In Alpine. They don't live there, but that's where they usually hang out on Sundays. Follow the directions closely. It'll take you to an observation point. They go in a different way and shouldn't see you."

I took the sheet and folded it in half. "Thank you."

"If you get names or anything else, I want it all," he said.

"No problem."

"And let someone know when you go."

I shoved the paper into my pocket. "Why?"

The eyes behind the glasses squinted at me and the lines around Gerald Famazio's mouth tightened. "Because there's a good chance you might not return."

25

I lay in bed all night thinking about Famazio's warning and the pins in his leg. My aches and pains were starting to subside. I'd been lucky that I'd survived my first two run-ins with Lonnie and Mo. I wondered who the third time would be the charm for.

I went for a run on the beach in the morning, the sunshine promising a warm day as it glistened off the ocean. For the first time in a while, the pain in my body was due more to exertion than to fighting.

I showered and was throwing on a pair of shorts and a T-shirt when my cell phone rang. I found it on the dining room table.

"Hello?"

"Where you at?" Carter asked, the line humming with music and a car engine.

"Home."

"Thought we might go make a run at Deacon Moreno."

It seemed like a month since I'd first heard Moreno's

name. I still hadn't come up with a reason for why Moreno would come after me, other than my looking for Linc.

"Okay. Where are you?"

"Just dropped Dana off," he said, and I could tell he was smiling.

"Jesus."

"She did mention something about me performing like the Messiah."

"I'll bet."

"I need something to eat before we go do this."

"Shocker."

"In-N-Out in Mission Valley?"

"Be there in half an hour."

I brought Carter up to speed while we ate. I told him about my meeting with Famazio and my overnight encounter with Lonnie and Mo, as well as my meeting with the Pluto aunt.

An hour later we were headed south on the 805 in my Jeep. He fidgeted uncomfortably in the passenger seat, tugging at his corduroy shorts and the chest of his Sex Waxx T-shirt like they didn't fit.

"What's wrong with you?" I asked.

"Nothing."

"Then why are you acting like you're a spaz?"

He glanced out his side window. "I'm getting impatient."

"We should be there in about fifteen minutes."

"No," he said. "Not Moreno. With these skinhead fucks."

"If you'd been at my place last night, I guess you would've been happy, then."

He ran a hand through his bright blond hair. "I'm not kidding, Noah." He turned to me. "They put you in the hospital once and you got lucky last night." His eyes hardened. "They gotta go, dude."

I glanced in the mirror and moved over a lane. "It'll happen."

"When?"

"Soon."

He shook his head and looked back out his window. I knew he wasn't satisfied with my answer, but I didn't have another one. Lonnie and Mo were on my list of things to take care of, but I needed to know where they fit in before making them a priority.

Just south of the zoo, we took Highway 94 east for several miles and exited at Euclid Avenue. We were in the heart of southeast San Diego, perhaps the most dangerous part of the city. Gangs, poverty, and indifference had made it a part of the metropolitan sprawl that most chose to ignore and avoid.

Willie, Carter's pal from the diner, had given him an Encanto address for Moreno, a small hillside neighborhood of low-slung houses surrounded by broken sidewalks and graffiti. Brown lawns, cracked asphalt, and broken windows were the dominant features of a community left for dead. In the late eighties, a kid named Sagon Penn had killed a cop with the cop's own gun during a traffic stop and Encanto had since become synonymous with violence.

Carter directed me through the side streets off Euclid until we hit Radio Drive. Moreno's house was in the middle of the block, a small square ranch painted a blue and gray that had probably been pleasant about fifteen years prior. A rusted-out Chevy Chevelle missing its hood was parked in the driveway, the small lawn next to it a mixture of brown grass and dirt. The iron bars on the windows practically screamed sad and hopeless.

I parked the Jeep across the street and looked at the house, completely devoid of the care you'd see in a home that people were proud to live in. Even my mother's house appeared more hospitable than this.

Carter glanced down the street. "How many houses are watching us right now, you think?"

I glanced down the street. "I saw curtains in two different windows move as we came down the street."

"So I say we double that and we're close."

Neighborhoods like this policed themselves and I knew they wouldn't take kindly to two outsiders showing up unannounced. We needed to be aware of what was going on around us.

I grabbed my 9mm Glock 17 from under my seat. "I'll take the house. You got the street?"

"Giant white guy hanging out in the driveway," he said, checking the magazine in his .45 HK Mark 23. "Think anyone'll notice?"

"Not if we get lucky."

He snapped the magazine back in place and racked the slide. "Can't remember the last time that happened."

I got out of the Jeep and Carter followed. He hung

back as I made my way up the drive and to the front door. The socket where the doorbell should've been was just a hole with wires. I rapped on the metal screen door.

A moment later, the doorknob twisted and I took a step back.

The door opened just enough for an attractive young girl to step into the opening and look at me. She looked to be nineteen or twenty, with light brown skin and striking amber-colored eyes. Her long black hair was cornrowed into thin tight braids that fell over her shoulder. She wore a red T-shirt and low-riding white cotton shorts.

She eyed me warily. "Yeah?"

"I'm looking for Deacon," I said.

"So?"

"Is he here?"

Her mouth twisted into a frown. "I look like his secretary or something?"

"I wouldn't know."

She sighed, annoyed. "Deacon ain't here."

"Know where I could find him?"

She leaned against the edge of the door, making no move to open the screen door between us. "Who're you?"

"I'm an investigator," I said.

"You don't seem like no cop."

"I'm not." I pulled a card out of my pocket and held it up. "I'm a private investigator."

She studied the card through the screen, then moved her eyes back to me, unimpressed. "What you want with my brother?"

I dropped the card back in my pocket. "Just want to ask him a few questions."

She looked past me, over my shoulder. "That big dude with you?"

I turned around to see Carter inspecting the beaten-down Chevelle in the driveway. "Yeah."

She blinked her eyes and ran a hand over her braids. "Think he gonna protect you if somebody come up on you?"

"Is that what's gonna happen?"

She snorted. "That's your own problem."

Good to know.

"I didn't know Deacon had a sister," I said, trying to sound friendly and unthreatening.

She thought about it, then nodded. "Yeah. I'm Malia."

"Malia, can you tell me where Deacon might be?"

"Deacon fuck you over or something?"

She kept answering my questions with her own and I tried to remain patient. "No. I just wanna ask him a couple questions."

"About what?"

"A case I'm working."

She sighed again and rolled her eyes. "Look, I know my big brother's a fuckup, alright? I know he does all kinds of shit with that gang of his." She shook her head. "Dumbass motherfucker that he is."

"You guys aren't close?"

She folded her arms across her chest. "Deacon's my brother. But I hate all this shit he's into. Gonna get himself done like the rest of these fools in this neighborhood. He's never going to get himself out of this place."

"What about you?" I asked. "Are you getting out?"

I heard more footsteps coming from behind the door and my hand slid around my back to my gun. Malia ducked behind the door and I heard a muffled exchange, but couldn't make out what was being said. She came back into the doorway.

Something had changed in her expression and she stood up a little straighter. "One more semester and I'm done at State. I'll have my degree and I'm outta here."

She saw my attention was on whoever was behind the door.

"And relax, dude," she said, shaking her head. "It ain't my brother in here. We're studying for a chemistry exam."

I watched the door, but nothing happened. I relaxed a little. "Chemistry?"

"I'm a physical science major."

We looked at each other for a long moment. I finally pulled the card out of my pocket again. "Can I give you this? You can pass it on to Deacon and tell him I'm looking for him."

"I ain't opening the screen," she said, her words firm. "I don't know you. Leave it outside and I'll get it after you go."

I stuck the card between the screen and the doorframe. "Fair enough."

"Don't count on him calling you," she said.

"He's not in trouble, Malia. At least not with me."

She smirked, looking at me like I'd just made some outrageous claim. "So you come into my neighborhood, this neighborhood, and expect me to believe Deacon ain't done nothin' wrong to get you here?" She laughed softly. "Nice try, mister."

"I just need to talk to him," I said.

"Noah," Carter called from behind me.

I turned around. He was focused on the end of the street. Three teenage boys were making their way toward us.

"You better go," Malia said, seeing them as well. She stepped back and shut the front door.

I walked down to the sidewalk to Carter. The boys were slowly ambling up the street, all of them dressed in baggy jeans and polo shirts, trying to look casual. They stopped when I joined Carter.

"Get anything?" he asked, not moving his eyes from our friends.

"Nothing."

"Man, you are so good at your job."

"Thanks."

The boys were now pretending to check out an old Cadillac parked on the street, engaged in an animated conversation. Their words didn't make it to us.

"The smart thing to do would be to get in your car and go," Carter said.

"Yes, it would."

"But you got nothing from the house."

"No, I didn't."

The vein in his neck pulsed. "So we gotta go talk to these guys, don't we?"

"Afraid so."

The conversation among the three stopped. They were about seventy-five yards away. They returned our stares.

Carter looked at me. "There may be more. In the houses. These guys may be decoys. I'll go behind you a little bit, so I can watch."

I nodded, the muscles in my back and stomach tightening. I flexed my trigger finger, knowing that it might get put to use.

"You ready?" Carter asked.

I wasn't, but it didn't matter.

We started walking.

26

The mild afternoon sun felt like a heat lamp on my neck as Carter and I walked down the street toward the boys. All three were about six feet tall, lanky, and athletic. Two had their heads shaved completely, the other an Afro that was teased nearly two feet off his head. The two shaved heads wore similar navy polos, the Afro a bright green one. The only difference I could see between the two shaved heads was that one of them had a gold hoop in each ear. The baggy jeans that they all sported looked designer. Their faces belied their tough-guy poses, though, and I put each of them at about fifteen years old.

"What's going on?" I asked, stopping a few feet short of them and trying to sound relaxed.

The kid with the Afro stepped forward and shrugged his shoulders. "Nothin', man. What's up with you?"

I couldn't think of anything better than the truth. "I'm trying to find Deacon."

The kid laughed, exposing a mouthful of white teeth. "Like you and he all tight and shit, right?"

The two boys behind him snickered.

"No," I said. "I just need to ask him some questions."

"You ain't no five-O," the one with the earrings said. " 'Cause you can't wear no shorts if you wearin' a badge."

"I'm an investigator."

The Afro lifted his chin and looked past me. "That your partner?"

"Something like that," I said, glad to know Carter was still behind me. "Any idea where I can find Deacon?"

The kid put a finger to his chin and pretended to think. "Hmmm."

"Hey, Carlos," the one without the earrings said. "I know where he might be."

Carlos smiled at me. "Where's that, Reg?"

Reg looked at me. "Mission Beach, man. He love it down there."

They all laughed. I did not.

Reg hit his twin in the shoulder. "Rudy, man. What's the name of that place he digs so much?"

Rudy grinned, a silver tooth in the middle of the grin. "Think it's called the SandDune or somethin' dumbass like that. Someplace you only find dumbass white dudes."

The anger percolated inside my body. They were sending a message. They wanted me to know that they had either been a part of or knew about the drive-by. The adrenaline spiked in my veins.

"Takes a lot of balls to shoot at somebody out of a car after asking for directions," I said. "You guys are real big-time. Deacon let you wipe his ass, too?"

The smiles disappeared. Carlos took a step toward me. "What you say, motherfucker?"

Carter, who was standing next to me, grunted. "What he said was, you guys are giant, and when I say giant, I mean *huge* pussies."

Fury raged in Carlos's eyes. "Hey, fuck you, Hulk Hogan."

"I'm not into guys, Carlos," Carter said. "Particularly ugly ones."

Carlos took another step forward and his hand went to his waistband. I lunged at him, grabbed him by the throat, swept his legs with one of mine, and dropped him onto his back.

"Anybody reaches any further and they get an extra hole to stick their finger in," Carter said, coming up next to me, his gun aimed at the two standing boys.

Reg moved his hand away from his body, but Rudy hesitated.

"You pull that thing out, bud, you better hope it's bigger than mine," Carter said to Rudy. "I'm fast and I don't miss."

Rudy stared at him for a moment, then eased his empty hand around to where it could be seen.

I looked down at Carlos, dug my knee into his chest, and pressed my right hand down on his throat. "You owe me."

Carlos's cool quickly evaporated. His eyes bulged and sweat formed on his forehead. "Bullshit."

"Bullshit? You come down to my neighborhood and shoot the place up? Try to kill me? Which part is bullshit?" I pressed harder on his chest.

"Man, you're chokin' him," Rudy said.

"Yeah, I am. And I'm gonna kill him if someone doesn't start talking." I smiled down at Carlos, squeezing his throat a little harder, his larynx feeling like a rock under my palm. "Right here in the street. In front of all your friends."

Carlos kicked his legs and slapped his arms wildly at my sides, all to no avail. He tried to speak, but I was cutting off the air and he gagged. His eyes darted from side to side, tears spilling out of the corners.

I looked up at his friends. "Somebody better start fucking talking."

They looked at each other, unsure what to do. They didn't want to be bullied, but they didn't want their leader to die, either. Their thug status was disappearing as reality turned them into scared kids.

"Deacon's over at Biddly's, man," Reg finally said, his voice a little higher than before.

I relaxed my grip slightly on Carlos's throat. "Keep talking."

"It's a liquor store," Reg said quickly. "Down on Euclid, past the school."

"Shit," Rudy whispered, clearly worried about the repercussions of giving up Deacon.

"He hang out there every day," Reg said, unable to stop himself now. "In the parkin' lot."

I looked back down at Carlos. Tears were running down his face. His chest fought for air beneath my knee. The fury that I'd seen in his eyes had been replaced by terror.

"You are one lucky fuck," I said to him.

"You two on the ground," Carter said. "Now."

Reg and Rudy dropped to the street on their stomachs. Carter walked over to them, removed their guns, and had them place their hands behind their backs. He dropped the small pistols in his pocket and walked back to me.

I took my hand off Carlos's throat, but kept my knee in his chest. "If I ever see you again, Carlos, I will finish this." I looked him right in the eye. "You understand?"

He couldn't stem the tears, but he gave a slight nod and turned his face away from mine.

I reached under him, removed the small handgun from his waistband, and stood up. "Roll over and place your hands on your back."

He did as I said.

Carter and I backed up quickly, not taking our eyes off them as we backpedaled toward the Jeep. The longer we stuck around, the bigger targets we became.

"I take it back," Carter said. "You are good at your job."

As we neared the Jeep, I saw Malia Moreno's face in the front window of the Moreno home. She was staring at us, her eyes wide in surprise.

I looked back down the street. None of the boys had moved, their faces still pressed to the asphalt.

I took a deep breath, trying to exhale the adrenaline

and anger that had taken over my body. The fingers that I had wrapped around Carlos's throat tingled.

"Let's go find Deacon," I said as we reached the Jeep. "Before he finds us."

27

The perspiration on my back glued my T-shirt to my seat as Carter and I drove to Biddly's.

"Think they'll try to beat us to Moreno?" I asked.

Carter shrugged. "Maybe, but probably not. They'll have to come up with a story about what happened first. They aren't gonna just tell him we took them down without a fight. On their street." He shook his head. "They'll just wait and hope Moreno kills us."

"Well, that makes me feel better."

"I'm like a living, breathing Hallmark card."

"Just like."

We turned left on Euclid. Half-empty strip malls lined the street, the traffic whizzing by them as if they didn't exist.

"Moreno won't be alone," I said.

"Not a fucking chance."

"Probably won't be as easy to shake as the teeny-boppers."

He pulled out the guns he'd taken off of Rudy and Reg. "But, gosh. We have all these."

I glanced at them. "Yeah, those should do the trick."

They were old, small pistols that resembled cap guns and were capable of doing about that much damage unless you had them stuck in someone's ear. I didn't think we'd be able to get that close to Deacon Moreno.

"You wanna dump these?" Carter asked.

I shook my head. "Not yet. Put them in the glove box. We'll toss them later."

He opened the box, slid them in, and shut the flap.

He tucked his own gun into the back of his waistband. "If Moreno was involved in the thing in front of the Dune, and I think we just learned he was, he's not gonna be surprised to see you." He paused. "If they set up that hit in Mission Beach and missed, they've probably been doing a little checking up on you."

I leaned forward, peeling the back of my shirt from the seat and letting Carter's observation settle into my gut like a sucker punch. It didn't feel good.

"So let's just ask him your questions," Carter said. "If we don't get the answers, we leave and figure out another way."

"Simple enough," I said, pulling the Jeep to the curb and knowing this was going to be anything but simple.

Biddly's was an old-time liquor store. A giant neon marquee hung over the street, the yellow and orange bulbs looking dim and faded in the daylight. A small parking lot separated the sign from the store by about a hundred feet, a rectangular building with bars on the windows that didn't hide the signs of the beer distributors. A pay phone and two newspaper bins stood to the right of the entrance. Just to the right of those was a metal sign proclaiming NO LOITERING. Sitting below the sign were three black guys in beach chairs, all in a row.

I got out of the Jeep and walked around to the sidewalk, next to Carter. The guy on the right end pulled out a cell phone, hit a button, stood up, and walked into the store.

"You gotta be kidding me," Carter said, staring at the two remaining guys.

"What?"

He blinked once, as if he were trying to confirm what he was seeing. I looked at the two in the chairs. They hadn't moved.

"What?" I repeated.

He shook his head. "Nothing. Tell you later."

"Okay," I said, puzzled.

Neither of the men stood up as we approached, just watched us as we moved closer. The one on the left was about six feet tall, thick with muscle. A thin scar ran across the bridge of his nose, white against his dark skin. Thin braids dangled from underneath a skin-tight black skullcap. Long arms extended from a dirty wife-beater tank and denim shorts covered most of his stretched-out legs, Nike running shoes on his feet. A plastic straw worked its way back and forth between his lips.

At first glance, he seemed barely awake. But even

though his eyes were only half open, I could see the pupils working back and forth in sync with the straw. Then his eyes shifted to Carter and stayed there.

The one on the right chuckled softly. "Well, well. Mr. Private Eye Man."

His acknowledgment of who I was didn't surprise me because I knew he was Moreno the second I saw his eyes. They were the same amber color as his sister's. Maybe a year or two older than his sister. His braids were similar to the other guy's, just fatter and shorter, with nothing else on his head. He was wearing a bright yellow Ralph Lauren button-down, tan slacks, and stark white Adidas high-tops. An expensive-looking watch hugged his wrist and an even more expensive gold chain hung off his neck.

But he didn't look worried.

"Moreno, right?" I said.

"Mr. Moreno to you," he said with more amusement than malice.

"Got some questions for you."

The door to the store opened and the kid who had gone in when we'd arrived stepped out. He looked at Moreno, gave a quick nod, and went back inside the store.

Moreno turned back at me and tilted his head to the side. "I'm not taking questions today."

"What day, then?"

"Not really sure."

He laughed at his own joke. The guy on the left just kept chewing the straw and staring at Carter. Carter held his gaze.

"You know Linc Pluto?" I asked anyway.

Moreno arched an eyebrow. "Nope."

"I think you do."

"Well, then you think wrong, white boy."

"Sometimes," I said. "But not this time. Met a guy who says you know him."

"Oh, yeah?" he said, raising both eyebrows. "Who's this guy that says I know Linc Pluto?" He smiled again. "Or whatever you said his name was."

"Doesn't matter," I said. "I don't care about the guns. I just wanna know about Pluto."

"Goodie-goodie for you," Moreno said, then laughed to himself again.

"Pluto work for you?"

He sat up a little in his chair and motioned to the guy next to him. "This here is Wesley. He handles all of our human resources shit." He grinned. "Whyn't you ask him?"

I looked at Wesley. "Pluto work for Moreno?"

Wesley ignored me, pulled the straw out of his mouth, and pointed it at Carter. "How's your jaw?"

"Fine," Carter said, his voice flat. "How're your ribs?"

"Fine." Wesley put the straw back in his mouth and started back to work on it.

They both tried to give off the feeling that their dialogue was casual, harmless. It seemed anything but that to me.

"Damn," Moreno said, looking back to me. "I guess human resources is closed today."

My irritation grew with his arrogance, but there

wasn't much I could do. We were on his turf and I had to be careful. I couldn't just throw him to the street like I had Carlos.

"Maybe I should just go back and ask Rudy and Reg," I said.

The grin on Moreno's face flickered down for a moment, but he caught himself quickly and tried to stay nonchalant.

"They're probably still lying in the street where we left them," I said. "Urine stains will be embarrassing when they stand up." I paused. "They promised us you'd be here, and damn if they weren't right."

The grin dissolved slowly this time and Moreno didn't bother trying to stop it. "That right?" He tilted his head to the side again. "I think it's time for you and the Great White Hope next to you to go."

"I'm not done yet," I said.

"Yes, you are," a voice said behind me.

Carter and I both turned. The guy matched Carter's height of six-nine and probably outweighed Carter by a hundred pounds. His skin was a deep black and wraparound shades hid his eyes on his boulderlike head. The white golf shirt and navy pants were funny attire for a guy aiming a TEC-9 machine gun at us.

A dark blue Ford Excursion with blacked-out windows and rims that shone like new money was idling quietly at the curb in front of my Jeep. The rear passenger door was open.

"Later, fellas," Moreno said, then laughed to himself one more time.

"Wizard's waiting," the huge man said.

I turned to Carter.

"Wizard's waiting," Carter said, and I thought I detected a small spark of excitement in his voice.

As we walked to the Excursion, I could find nothing exciting about going to meet Wizard Matellion.

28

The interior of the Excursion resembled a mobile nightclub. Instead of the standard passenger seats, there was a leather bench running along the walls. A square oak table filled the middle, a bottle of Crown Royal sitting inside the brass rails that rimmed it. Pungent cologne permeated the air like it was being piped through the vents. The stereo system, even turned down, sounded expensive and ear-busting. The windows were blacked out and theater lighting dotted the ceiling.

Carter and I slid onto the seats that faced the rear of the vehicle, a dark partition behind our heads preventing us from seeing who was driving. The Jolly Black Giant with the TEC-9, who had patted us down and removed our guns before we got within ten feet of the car, climbed in behind us and occupied the space next to Wizard Matellion.

Wizard sat in the back corner. He had dark chocolate

skin with closely cropped black hair. Around six feet tall, athletic build, and a friendly smile on his dark face. He wore a bright blue nylon Adidas warm-up suit zipped up to his chin. White high-tops covered his feet.

He extended his hand toward me, thick gold bands on his fingers flashing. "I'm Wizard."

I shook his hand. "I think you know my name."

He nodded and extended his hand toward Carter. Carter didn't move, keeping his eyes on the giant. Wizard's smile tightened a little as he withdrew his hand and sat back in his seat. He motioned to the giant. "This is Ollie."

Ollie didn't move, keeping his eyes on Carter.

The engine hummed a little louder and we glided away from the curb.

"Sorry to have to meet like this," Wizard said. "But I gotta be careful going out in public."

"So many friends," I said.

He laughed. "Yes. So many friends." He waved a hand in front of him. "I don't want to keep you for too long. For future reference, it might be better if you contacted me before you came down to this neighborhood."

His casual tone made him sound like a Realtor speaking to potential home buyers. But that tone didn't make me forget that he killed people for a living.

"We'll remember that," I said. "But to be honest, we were just looking to talk to Deacon."

"Deacon works for me."

"I know that."

His smile widened. "Then you probably know the

game, so you knew you were gonna have to talk to me first anyway before Deacon would talk to you."

"Nothing goes down without your approval?"

"I'm like the CEO."

"So did you order Moreno to take me out?"

The grin didn't falter. "Sometimes Deacon likes to pretend he's management, going and doing his own thing. It's called initiative." His white teeth gleamed in the dark interior. "So I'm not sure what you're talking about. I'll have to talk to him about that."

I nodded. "Sure."

He leaned back in his seat. "Is that all you wanted with Deacon?"

The rhythm of the wheels on the pavement came through my seat. "No."

"What else, then?"

"I wanted to know if he knows a kid named Linc Pluto."

Matellion crossed one leg over the other. "Name doesn't sound familiar to me."

"Deacon was working with him."

"Deacon say so?"

I shook my head.

Wizard shrugged. "Then maybe you're wrong."

I glanced at Carter. He and Ollie were smiling at one another, each silently daring the other to do something.

I looked back at Wizard. "Let me put this another way. Deacon Moreno was working with Linc Pluto, who I think is a white supremacist."

The grin finally faltered and the charming façade

that Wizard Matellion worked so hard at began to crumble.

"White supremacist?" he said, his voice an octave lower than before. "Fuckin' skinhead and shit?"

"Something like that."

"And you're telling me Deacon is tight with him?"

I nodded.

Wizard thought about that for a moment, then shook his head. "Bullshit."

"Got someone who says it was happening."

"Someone you believe?"

I didn't know who I believed, but at least I had Wizard interested.

"Yeah," I said.

Wizard fiddled with one of the rings on his fingers, staring hard at it. He looked back at me. "Why you looking for this Pluto dude?"

"Because someone hired me to look for him," I said, starting to feel claustrophobic. I leaned forward toward Matellion. "Mind if I ask another question?"

The smile came back and the bright white teeth flashed. "Go ahead."

"Let me start with what I know," I said. "I know I was hired to find Linc Pluto, who had something to do with some sort of hate group. I know that his older brother was killed, probably by the same group."

I watched for a reaction, but didn't get one.

"At the same apartment complex where Deacon used to live, a girl who lives next door to Pluto gets shot. Shortly after that, some of your guys paid me a visit in my neighborhood. So here's my question."

Wizard folded his arms across his chest, but didn't look away.

I leaned forward a little more. "Why did your guys try to take out the girl at the apartment?"

Ollie directed the TEC-9 at my nose, but I didn't take my eyes off Wizard. After a moment, Wizard reached out and pushed the gun away and back toward Carter.

Carter didn't seem to notice.

"I don't do no business with no fuckin' skinheads, dude," Wizard said quietly.

"That doesn't answer my question." I paused. "Why the girl?"

I knew there was a connection between Linc and Moreno. Rachel, while living next door to Linc, had been shot at a place where Moreno used to live. I learned early in my career that coincidence was for people who liked to ignore the facts.

"I don't know anything about this girl," he said finally, shaking his head.

"Then why did your guys come after me?" I asked. "Right after I talked with her?"

"Probably because you were sticking your nose where it shouldn't be."

"Probably?" I said, almost laughing. "I'd think the *CEO* would have a better handle on things in his own *company*."

Wizard's arms tightened across his chest. "You think that because you're big and white, I'm just gonna tell you some shit?" He tilted his head. "Even if I did know the answers, what do I get out of all this?"

"I don't know and I don't care," I said. "But I just

wonder how all your friends—and for that matter, your employees—would feel about you if they knew you were doing business with some skinheads."

Wizard Matellion's friendliness disappeared completely. He nudged Ollie slightly and for a moment I thought he was telling him to shoot me.

But Ollie just reached up with his free hand and knocked twice on the ceiling.

The car moved to the right and glided to a stop.

"I'll be in touch," Wizard said. "Now get out."

Ollie opened the door and exited first. Carter and I followed him out into the bright sunlight.

Ollie opened up the front passenger door and produced our guns. He laid them on the sidewalk near the front of the car. Then he walked back and climbed into the Excursion

"Braddock?" Matellion said.

I looked back in the SUV.

"Don't come into my neighborhood again without asking," he said, his eyes staring out at me like hard spikes. Then he flashed the grin from before. "Because next time, you won't walk out alive."

29

"You believe him?" Carter asked, stretching out on one of the plastic resin chairs on my patio.

We had made our way back to Biddly's after Wizard kicked us out. Moreno and Wesley were gone from their perch in front of the liquor store and, with Wizard's warning fresh in our heads, we drove back to Mission Beach and settled under the hazy late-day sunshine.

I yanked the caps off two Red Trolley Ales and handed Carter one as I sat down in the chair next to him. "Yes and no."

He put the bottle to his lips and waited for me to continue.

"I think he knew about the hit down here," I said, squinting into the orange and yellow hues above the water. "Something like that, no way it happens without his okay. They had two cars with at least four guys. It was organized. That was crap about Moreno and his initiative."

Carter nodded. "It's a smart play on his part. He may have known who we were, but he doesn't know if we're tied to cops or feeding somebody info on him. He admitted nothing, basically."

"I think he knew about Rachel, too," I said, watching two bicyclists cruise by on the boardwalk, the bike tires sounding like zippers on the pavement. "He may not have known why, but I think he knew it happened."

"Why did they go after her?"

"I'm not sure," I said, frustrated that I hadn't been able to come up with an answer for that. "Maybe they thought she told me something."

"Nah, man, that doesn't make sense. You'd just talked to her. How could they have put that together so quickly?"

He was right. I was starting to think that I had the reasoning backward. I'd been operating under the idea that Rachel had been shot because I'd talked to her. But it was beginning to look more like I'd been attacked at the SandDune because I'd witnessed her shooting by coincidence.

I drank from the beer and then set it on the table between us. "I don't think he was lying about Moreno and Linc, though."

"You mean that he didn't know they had something going?"

"I think he knew something was happening. Would seem reasonable that he lets Moreno buy from whomever. But I don't think he knew exactly who Moreno was dealing with. You see his reaction? It was the only time he stumbled. And he was pissed."

He nodded. "Yeah, he didn't seem too happy about having an association with the California coalition of white sheets. And if that's what was going on—Moreno buying from Pluto—Matellion is not gonna like how that looks, even if Moreno didn't know that Pluto was a hater. In which case, you may have just ended Deacon Moreno's life."

I nodded, not really feeling one way or another about that possibility. I found it hard to drum up sympathy for someone who had been an active participant in trying to end my life. If he wanted to work for Wizard Matellion, he would have to live with the consequences.

I remembered the scene outside the liquor store. "What was that shit with you and Wesley?"

A slow grin emerged on Carter's lips as he pulled the bottle away from his mouth. "About a year ago, I was doing some recovery work for a guy in Tucson."

"Recovery work?"

"Finding a guy who owed my guy some money," he said, waving the bottle in the air. "You don't wanna know. I go down to Ensenada to find this guy and the guy that hired me says another dude's meeting me there, in case I need some help." He smirked. "I was polite and didn't tell him that wouldn't be necessary."

"Big of you."

"Very. Guess who my help was."

"Wesley?"

"Yep. Met him at the house where the dude was hiding." He shrugged. "We exchange hellos and then we go into the house, grab the dude, and lucky us, we find a big-ass duffel bag of money, too."

"Lucky."

"So we do our thing with the guy and I grab the bag of cash to take back to my employer." He shook his head, his eyes somewhere on the horizon. "Then old Wesley grabs it from me, says that *my* boss actually owes *his* boss and that's why he took the job."

"Wizard?" I asked.

"I guess," Carter said. "I didn't know it at the time, but that makes sense now. So he wants the money, says he's taking it with him." His mouth slithered into a grin. "And I said no."

Carter raised the bottle to his lips and drained it, then set the bottle down on the table.

"I drilled him in the ribs and put him on his ass and he dropped the bag," he said, still smiling. "I know I broke a couple of them because I felt those fuckers crack. Then I bend over to pick up the bag and he catches me flush in the jaw with his foot."

"Oops."

He rubbed his jaw. "I had to get two teeth put back in. Anyway, we heard sirens, figured the *federales* were on their way, and got the hell out of there." He paused. "And I, of course, left with the money."

"Of course."

"Hadn't seen or heard from the guy until today."

I shook my head. Carter lived in a comic-book world that the rest of us thought couldn't possibly be real. He enjoyed proving otherwise.

"Great story, but none of it helps me," I said.

"You asked, and I didn't say it would."

The more I worked over what we'd learned, the

more I thought Moreno had made a simple mistake. He knew a guy who could supply him with guns. But he hadn't checked him out. If he had known that Linc was tied to National Nation, he probably would've flat-out tried to kill him.

Carter sat up in the chair. "Dollar drafts down at the Pennant tonight. Wanna go over?"

"Dollar drafts?" I said, a tiny bell going off in my brain. "That would mean today's Saturday."

"Uh, yeah. All day, I think."

The pounding in my head turned into an ugly jackhammer.

I stood up. "I can't."

"Why not?"

I watched the sun fight with the horizon, trying to squeeze out a few more minutes of daylight before it disappeared for another night. I stared at it for a moment, watching the water swallow the last few rays, silently pleading with the water to take me as well.

"Because," I finally said, wishing hard that it were already Sunday, "I'm having dinner with Carolina Braddock."

30

Carter left without saying much, knowing that my anxiety level was skyrocketing by the second.

I changed into a pair of shorts and a collared Quiksilver pullover and headed out. I walked up Mission to the small Italian restaurant I'd told Carolina about on my message. I'd been standing out front for about fifteen minutes, wondering if she'd gotten my message, when she came strolling up the sidewalk.

She wore a yellow-and-white-striped cotton sundress, her hair falling on her bare shoulders. A simple gold watch on one wrist and a matching bracelet on the other. White leather sandals glowed against her tan feet.

"You found it," I said.

"I did." She hesitated for a moment. "I was surprised at your message. I thought we were going to have dinner at your home."

"Nah," I said, putting a hand on her arm and guiding her toward the door of the restaurant. "This'll be better."

I avoided her look. I knew she was thinking I was keeping her out of my life. But I didn't feel like explaining that we might be in danger at my place.

"Whatever you say," she said.

The hostess took us to a table on the restaurant's patio that faced the boardwalk.

As Carolina walked by me to her chair, I reflexively sniffed the air for alcohol, but came up empty.

"You live so close to the water," she said. "What a wonderful view you must have."

"Yeah, it's not bad."

"You always did love the beach."

"Yep."

The waitress arrived at our table. "Can I get you all something to drink?"

"Water's fine," Carolina said without looking at me.

"Me, too."

The waitress disappeared.

"You've lived down here a long time, haven't you?"

"Since college."

She nodded, as if she knew that already. She turned to me. "I should've come down to see you."

I shrugged, not wanting to get angry.

"I should be familiar with my son's home," she said.

The waitress came back with our water and we ordered our food.

After she'd been gone for a few minutes, Carolina said, "I'm sorry."

I sipped the water. "Don't be."

A faint smile appeared on her lips. "Thank you."

"I didn't do anything."

"Thank you for inviting me here, Noah," she clarified, her thin eyebrows rising just slightly. "For inviting me to your home. Or at least, to where you live."

I looked across the table at her. As far as I could tell, she arrived sober and she was making an effort. I was straddling the line somewhere between indifferent and asshole, and that probably wasn't fair.

"You're welcome," I said.

When our food came, we ate quietly, the clinks of the silverware on the plates interspersed with the soft falling of the waves out beyond the boardwalk. The silence brought back memories of quiet evening meals when I was growing up, as Carolina more often than not was suffering through a hangover after an alcohol-drenched day. I managed to quell the anger and bitterness that threatened to spill out of my mouth, trying to simply enjoy the moment for what it was.

After we finished, she ordered coffee and we sat there in the still evening air.

"How is your job?" she asked, her voice sounding foreign after the long period of silence.

"It's good," I answered. "I like my boss."

"Who's that?"

"Me."

She smiled. "Of course." Her smile faded to concern. "You wouldn't tell me about the bruises on your face the other day."

"It's no big deal."

"Do you get hurt often?"

"I try not to," I said. "But sometimes it happens."

Her hazel eyes focused intently on me, as if she were trying to figure out where a puzzle piece was meant to fit. "You were always tough. Even as a boy."

I didn't say anything, not knowing whether her statement was a compliment or criticism.

"But I guess you didn't really have a choice," she said. "I made that choice for you."

I stared at the black edge of the water, trying to find the waves. "Yeah, probably."

She shifted in the chair and I felt her eyes leave me.

"I'm sorry," she said.

"I know," I said.

"And I'm sorry that I'm always saying I'm sorry," she said, her voice catching just slightly. "I wanted it to be different. I always did, but I could never get it right." She paused. "I'd look at you and know that I was screwing up, but I just couldn't fix it. I wanted to, you may not have known that, but I did." She turned back to me. "And then you were eighteen and gone. My tough little boy out of my house and out of my life."

I looked at her, not necessarily surprised by the words, but maybe by the sincerity. I remembered leaving the house the summer after I graduated from high school. I managed to talk my way into the dorms early at San Diego State, negotiating a move-in right after the Fourth of July. I'd taken two surfboards and a duffel bag full of clothes. I left the rest behind, not needing or wanting anything else out of that house or that life. I'd seen her twice since that day, both times inadvertent and uncomfortable.

"I am sorry, Noah," she said, her voice catching again. "I really am."

"I know."

"I'm not asking to come back into your life," she said. Then she laughed, the lines around her eyes tightening. "That's a lie. That's exactly what I'm asking for. But not all at once. I don't want to come in and try to make up for lost time, for the years that I failed you. I can't and I know that." She stopped for a moment, then reached across the table and put her hand on my arm. "I just want to know my son again."

I looked at her hand on my arm, surprised that I hadn't pulled away. Her nails were neatly manicured and it was one of those obscure things that takes you back to childhood. I had loved the smell of nail polish as a kid and I remembered sitting next to her as a seven- or eight-year-old while she painted her nails.

"I can't do the drinking thing," I said, still looking at her hand. "I just can't."

"I haven't had a drink since you brought me home the other day," she said.

It wasn't defensive and it wasn't angry. She was just letting me know. And I'm not sure whether it was the clarity in her eyes or the sincerity of what I was hearing or the memory of the nail polish.

But I believed her.

I moved my eyes from her hand to her face. When she had come up the alley, I thought she looked as young as she always had. But up close, I could see the fine wrinkles on her face, the faint gray in her hair, and the exhaustion of someone much older in too many ways.

She wouldn't be there forever.

"Alright," I said.

She tilted her head, tiny tears in the corners of her eyes. "Alright?"

If she could try to give up the alcohol, I could try to give up the bitterness.

"The bruises," I said. "I got them from a guy named Mo. And he's the reason we're at this restaurant rather than my place."

I saw the tension that she'd been carrying in her shoulders since she arrived slowly inch away. She blinked twice, like she was making sure that whatever invisible barrier had been between us was gone. "Mo."

I nodded and spent the rest of the night letting my mother get to know her son again.

We walked back down Mission to where Carolina had parked her car and she left a little before eleven, before either of us had time to say or do something stupid and ruin the evening. I told her I'd call her in a day or two. No hugs, no kisses, no stiff gestures or insincere affection between us. Just small smiles, quick nods, and the hope that maybe we could figure out how to be something close to mother and son again.

I slept well for what seemed like the first time in months—my need for sleep finally overruling any concerns I had about skinheads, gang members, or Plutos—and woke up early with a clear head. I hadn't checked in on Rachel in a while and called the hospital. She answered on the third ring. I was relieved to hear that she was doing fine—her shoulder was still sore, but she was healing. She told me that she was leaving later in the day—her parents were coming to pick her up and she was going to stay with them for a little while. I gave her my cell-phone number and told her to call me if she needed anything and then said goodbye.

I sat on my sofa for a few minutes, wondering if I could've done anything else for Rachel. I still didn't understand how she was connected to everything, what she'd done to make someone shoot her. The more I thought about it, the more confused I got. Frustrated by the lack of any concrete answers, I finally gave up, pulled on my trunks, grabbed the Ron Jon, and headed out for the water.

The water was smooth and the waves were solid, rolling in at regular intervals, letting me work up a rhythm of riding and paddling back out, my muscles loosening with each movement. I was sharp, gliding down the faces, snapping through the lips, floating on the tops. It was effortless and it felt good. I lasted for about an hour beneath a clear sky and a bright early morning sun and I couldn't help but smile as I walked back up the sand to my place.

I showered, dressed, and called Carter.

He answered with a grunt.

"You up?" I asked.

"Am now."

"You missed good water this morning."

"Seriously?"

"Yep."

"Dammit."

"Definitely sucks for you. Can you be over here in about an hour?"

I heard him stifle a yawn. "For the right price."

"Breakfast will do?"

"Affirmative."

"I need you to bring a couple things," I said.

I told him what they were.

The line buzzed for a moment, then he said, "I'm assuming you'll explain when I get there?"

"I will."

"Breakfast better be hot."

Forty-five minutes later I was wrapping the chorizo and scrambled eggs into tortillas when Carter strode in the door.

"I'll assume there are at least three of those for me," he said, his electric-white hair still wet, a wrinkled yellow T-shirt and long cargo shorts covering his frame. "I could eat a fat man."

"Fortunately, the fat men will be safe today," I said, placing two of the burritos on a plate and sliding it across the counter. "Two more for you when you're ready."

He sat down at the kitchen table, wolfed one down in three bites, and was halfway through the second when he asked, "How was last night?"

I sat down across from him. "Good."

"Just good?"

I thought about it. "Yeah."

The second burrito was gone and he walked into the kitchen to grab a third. "Yelling, screaming, any of that?"

"None."

He came back and sat down again. "Wow. Sounds like you acted like an adult."

"Shut up."

He shrugged and started in on the burrito. I knew he was right, but I didn't want to discuss my mother. If I started talking and thinking more about her and our dinner, I knew I'd start second-guessing myself and doubting Carolina. I needed to just let it sit and see what happened.

Carter wiped his mouth with the back of his hand. "Thanks. That was good."

I stared at his empty plate. "Did you even taste them?"

"A little bit," he said, pushing back from the table and stretching out his legs. "So. Wanna tell me what we're doing today?"

"You bring everything?"

He nodded. "A couple of rifles, scopes, and a bunch of ammo. We going on some sort of man picnic?"

"You wish," I said, standing up from the table and grabbing both of our plates.

"You aren't gonna break out a ring and propose to me, are you?" he asked, his eyebrows bouncing up and down.

I walked into the kitchen and dumped the plates in the sink. "I might propose you go screw yourself."

"I've heard that before."

"No doubt," I said. "We're going out to Alpine."

He made a face like I'd said we were going to go eat sewage instead of going to one of the outermost areas of San Diego County.

"Alpine?" he said, practically spitting the word out. "Why not just go to Kansas? Almost as far east."

"I'm trying to expand your cultural horizons."

"Gonna have to take me a lot fucking farther than Alpine to do that."

"Well, then, that's not a trip I ever wish to make."

He shook his head, then twisted around in his chair to look at me as I walked by him out to the kitchen. "Why are we wasting a perfectly good day going to Alpine, Noah?"

I stared past him out the glass door at the water. He was right. It was a perfectly good day. The light blue sky over the dark blue water made for a pretty picture.

I didn't know if it was because of my renewed optimism over my relationship with Carolina, but I was feeling more of a sense of urgency to solve the whole Pluto thing. Linc was the one who could thread all of it together. I'd agreed to his aunt's request to continue looking for him, but in truth, I was doing it more for me than for her. Mo and Lonnie had already made one visit to my home. I didn't want another where someone other than me might have to face their wrath. And I refused to be glancing behind me, watching for them.

I reached for my gun on the counter. I checked the chamber and racked the slide, the noise echoing off the living room walls.

"We are going to Alpine," I said, staring hard at the door, the brand-new glass door that had replaced the old one. "Because it's time to go visit Lonnie and Mo."

Brochures handed out by the Chamber of Commerce would have you believe that all of San Diego looks out upon sparkling blue ocean or a harbor dotted with sailboats. A carefree place to visit where everyone has a view of the ocean.

While that is true for the fortunate few who live on the coastline, most of San Diego County is made up of communities set in canyons, hills, and brush that can't get a sniff of the ocean even on the best day. Thirty miles to the east, Alpine is one of those places.

Interstate 8 snaked us through Mission Valley, north of San Diego State and then out to La Mesa and El Cajon. The highway then elevated up into the small mountain communities near Descanso and Julian, areas that were regularly singed with brush fires every summer, but managed to make comebacks as soon as the flames were extinguished.

The map that Professor Famazio had given me led

us to an area just east of Alpine, on the western edge of Cleveland National Forest, before the interstate dropped again and made its way out to El Centro and the scorched desert of Arizona.

"We should let Arizona annex this part of San Diego," Carter observed, shaking his head. "Tell 'em to send over a few fine-looking ladies from the U of A with a case of beer and it's theirs."

"Type that up and send it to the governor," I said, pulling off the highway and heading north. "Never know what might happen."

He nodded, as if the thought had never occurred to him. "I think I'll do that."

The two-lane asphalt road took us higher into the dense forest, the tall green pines hovering over the road and smothering the air with their aroma. We crested the highest point and started to descend through a series of S-curves. Famazio's directions indicated a turnoff at the middle of the curves and I found it on our right, easing the Jeep into it, the tires crunching on the gravel.

"We gotta walk a little from here," I said, opening my door.

"I better get to shoot someone," Carter grumbled.

I walked around to the back of the Jeep. "No promises."

He came around to meet me. "I wasn't asking for permission."

"You shoot anybody without my permission and it is a long walk back to Mission Beach."

He stuck his tongue out at me.

We pulled his gear out of the back of the Jeep. The rifles were Ruger Mini-30s. Each had a scope attached to it. I noticed a selector switch on each receiver.

"I thought these were semiautomatics," I said.

"They were," he said, laying his on his shoulder. "Originally."

"You had them converted to fully automatic? That legal?"

He shrugged. "Yeah. Sorta. I don't know."

I shook my head.

We divvied up the magazines and walked down a dirt path that led from the turnout. It was steep and narrow and uncomfortable, our feet sliding forward on the loose rocks and uneven terrain every few steps. After ten minutes of walking and sliding, the path leveled off and then disappeared amid a cluster of pines.

"Now where?" Carter asked.

I looked at the map. "Should be right here."

I moved forward to the trees and saw that about four trees in, the earth dropped away. I heard muffled voices down below.

"This is it," I said, lowering my voice. I motioned to our right. "Let's move up here, off the end of the trail."

We went about ten yards off the trail and found a wider spot between two of the pines at the edge and lay down on our stomachs, putting the guns between us. We inched carefully toward the edge of the landing and looked down.

The area was a hundred feet below us, maybe twenty square yards of dirt and trodden grass. A concrete fire ring was the center of the circular patch. A boom box sat next to the ring, speed metal blaring from the speakers. At the farthest edge of the circle, the front ends of a couple of pickup trucks poked out from just behind the trees. A cache of assault rifles was spread out on the ground near the trucks. A thin trail disappeared into the trees next to the trucks, indicating another entry point.

About a dozen guys lounged in various acts of slackerdom—several in low-slung lawn chairs, a couple shaking their heads to the music, a few more standing, holding cans of beer. They all wore some variation of camouflage pants, white T-shirts, army jackets, and black leather boots.

All of them had one thing in common.

A shaved head.

"Cool," Carter whispered. "A party."

"And we didn't get invites."

"Probably 'cause we go to the wrong barber."

We were too high up to make out any of the words in the muffled conversations below us. An occasional laugh drifted up to us, but that was it.

"Can I just pick 'em off?" Carter asked. "One by one?"

"That would probably be Plan Z."

"What's Plan A?"

"We lie here and see what happens."

He glanced at me. "You are so boring."

"One of my best qualities."

"Said the really boring guy."

"Shut up."

Carter scanned the area. "See your guys anywhere?"

"Nope."

"How much am I getting paid for this?"

"Same as always."

He paused. "You've never paid me before."

"Exactly."

He dropped his head to the tarp and closed his eyes. "Wake me when I can turn this place into a shooting gallery."

Ten minutes later, he was snoring softly, earning every cent of what I wasn't paying him.

I watched what went on down below. They stuck together in groups of two or three, talking, laughing, occasionally goofing off with a shove or a fake punch. Most of them appeared to be in their early twenties and it easily could've been mistaken for a frat party.

Except for their cue-ball heads and the pile of guns.

After an hour of squinting to make out their tattoos, counting the empty beer cans, and stacking close to a hundred pine needles on Carter's cheek, I was ready to give up.

I pushed back from the ledge and sat up, stretching the numb muscles in my back and arms. I started to stand up to unkink my legs when I heard a couple of shouts down below and what sounded like the hum of a car engine.

I dropped down to my stomach and slid back to the ledge.

The group was moving slowly over to the area of trees where the trucks were parked. The front end of another vehicle nosed up next to the ones I'd seen before.

My shoulders stiffened as Lonnie emerged from the truck and walked into the circle.

He high-fived several of the guys as a greeting, smiling and nodding confidently.

I pulled one of the Ruger rifles closer to me.

I reached over and punched Carter in the arm. "Hey."

He lifted his head up with a start, then frowned as the pile of pine needles fell off his face and down around his shirt collar.

He started brushing them off. "What?"

I nodded down at the campground. "Guy in the black T-shirt. That's one of them."

The anger that had visited me twice before when I'd encountered Lonnie was knocking in my stomach.

Carter stared down below for a moment. "Where's the other guy?"

My fingers tingled. "Haven't seen Mo yet."

The way Lonnie interacted with his buddies, the way he moved among them, the way they all wanted to say hello to him, it was clear that he was a leader.

I reached out and placed my hand on the rifle.

"Hang on," Carter said, now fully awake, reacting to my movement. "Let's see what goes down."

Lonnie threw his head back, his laugh working into the air and up to us. I could see black stitching across his nose, courtesy of my having slammed it into the floor at my house.

My hand closed around the rifle's stock.

Lonnie turned back toward the trucks and the trees.

"Dude," he yelled. "Come on." There was more laughter in the group.

Carter glanced at me. I looked at him and shrugged. Then I focused back to the trees as a movement caught my attention.

Mo emerged from the pines, a sort of neo-Nazi Bigfoot. He wore a sleeveless black T-shirt, his arms bulging with muscle. A bandage poked out of the shirt near his shoulder where I'd shot him. The canvas pants on his lower half hugged his tree-trunk-like legs.

"Fuck," Carter said. "He is big."

Mo was pulling a rope. It was taut and angled down toward the ground as if it were tied to something.

Lonnie motioned for him to hurry up, excitedly, to keep pulling the rope.

"He go deer hunting or something?" Carter asked. "What the hell's he got on the end of that?"

I watched.

Mo tugged on the rope and glanced behind him. Then he looked back toward the group, leaned forward a little, and started pulling the rope like a trained mule.

I could make out something at the end, sliding heavily through the tree trunks and pine needles.

The group started whooping and hollering, celebrating like a team that had just won a championship.

The end of the rope came into view and I felt myself rising up on my elbows, my mind not believing what it was seeing, my hand clamping down on the rifle.

"Motherfucker," Carter whispered.

They had gone hunting, alright.

Hands bound, gagged at the mouth, Mo's rope tied tightly around her ankles, Malia Moreno was their trophy.

33

"Is that Moreno's sister?" Carter asked, his voice edged with surprise.

"Yeah," I said, the muscles at my neck coiling into knots as I slid my eye to the scope for a closer look.

Malia's eyes were wide, fear radiating from them. Dirt caked the sides of her face, held there by streams of tears. Blood leaked out of her nose and the corners of her mouth. She was wearing a tank top and one of the straps had been torn. She wasn't fighting Mo or the rope, her body sliding along the ground like a bag of sand.

"We gotta get closer," I said, sliding back and rising to my knees.

Carter pushed away from the ledge and popped to his feet like he was riding his surfboard. "Work from opposite sides?"

I nodded, reaching for one of the rifles. "Try to stay just above them. I'll get to the ground and take the ones closest to her. You take the others. Try to herd them to their trucks and get them to run."

He grabbed the remaining rifle, stuffed several of the extra magazines into his pockets, pivoted, and disappeared into the trees.

I took the rest of the magazines and moved quickly through the trees in the opposite direction and down the slope, staying close enough to the edge to monitor the campground.

Malia was near the fire ring now, the skinheads in a semicircle around her. She was attempting to move, rolling around like a wounded insect. Several of the skinheads moved toward her like they were going to kick her, then held up at the last second, laughing as she tried to roll out of reach. Mo dropped the rope and headed to the back of the crowd.

When I reached level ground, I was about twenty-five yards away from Malia and the assholes.

"Boys, check it out," Lonnie said, standing near Malia's head. "Got ourselves a pretty little porch monkey here."

Their cheers and jeers melded together, exploding into the air.

Lonnie squatted down. "And there's nothing I like better than putting a motherfucking little porch monkey out of her misery."

I lay down behind a thick pine, my left shoulder pressed into the trunk, the pine needles sticking me in the elbows, and got the Ruger Mini-30 in position. I felt my chest heaving and took a couple of deep breaths to steady myself. We were outnumbered and I knew that even with both Carter and myself armed, we were going to have a hard time gaining control of the situation.

"Hey, Lonnie. We get a shot at her before we off her?" somebody asked from the group.

I checked the magazine.

"You know? Do her before we do her?" The guy stepped over Malia. He was tall and thin, black suspenders holding up his camouflage pants over his dirty white T-shirt. "Show the bitch what she's gonna miss?"

Lonnie stood up and laughed as the group screamed its approval.

I felt my breathing level out, my hands relaxing on the rifle.

Malia's body bucked in the dirt, the group roaring again at her movement, epithets ringing into the air.

The thin guy pulled his suspenders off his shoulders, straddled Malia, and dropped to his knees.

I adjusted my eye to the scope and brought the guy's torso into focus, and took a deep breath.

"What do you think, nigger?" he asked, his lips curled into an arrogant sneer. "Want a little of me?"

I exhaled and squeezed the trigger.

The thin guy jerked back, a small red puff popping out of his chest, and fell off Malia.

I took another deep breath, trying to get the action to slow down in front of me.

Two more fell to the ground near him, shots coming from the far side of the campground.

Panic set in. Some dove for the ground and some ran

for their guns, screaming and yelling, their heads swiveling in both directions. Lonnie dropped to the ground, obscured by the fire ring. My shots skimmed over him.

The guns near the trucks came to life and fired toward Carter's side. I shifted to my left and fired in that direction and saw several of the shooters scatter farther into the cover of the pines.

We'd caught them unorganized and unprepared and it showed.

More yelling, then bullets whistling over my head and off to my right. My muscles tightened, involuntarily trying to make my body smaller. I wanted to move, but I would be too exposed.

The two that Carter shot were being dragged away, two guys firing pistols from near the trucks to cover themselves. The one I'd hit was still down next to Malia, not moving.

I couldn't see Lonnie.

Heavy gunfire erupted from near the trucks. Mo was kneeling just inside the tree line, firing what looked like an AK-47 in Carter's direction.

I fired twice at Mo. The first one missed, the second one caught him in the thigh.

It didn't faze him. He shifted to his left, got his body behind one of the trees, and kept firing.

More shots came from our original position up on the ledge, aimed at Mo. I jerked my head in that direction, surprised and confused. I couldn't make out anyone up on the plateau and wondered who in the hell might be helping us.

Mo moved to a crouch and returned the fire up on the ledge.

A shot boomed from near the fire ring, a large-caliber handgun burst, and Lonnie was up and running low toward the tree line. Mo rotated and fired at me, covering him. I tucked in tight behind the trunk of the pine, my forehead scraping against the bark. Bullets thudded into the trees around me, wood chips showering my neck and face.

The truck engines revved to life, drowning out the screams for the rest to hurry.

Mo waited for the last of his buddies to get into the tree line, then limped back quickly, still sweeping the entire outer edge of the campground with the AK-47. He disappeared into the trees.

Doors slammed, tires spewed rocks and dirt through the trees, and the trucks U-turned and headed out to wherever they'd come from.

The entire skirmish had taken maybe two minutes.

The quiet was overwhelming.

"You good?" Carter yelled from the other side of the circle.

I couldn't see him. "Yeah. You?"

"Yeah."

I moved from my stomach to my knees, my throat aching and burning from the gun smoke and dirt.

Malia was still next to the fire ring, her would-be rapist beside her.

Carter emerged from the trees across from me. His rifle was aimed up at our original spot.

I rose to my feet and walked slowly toward the fire

ring, holding the rifle at a ready position and watching the entire tree line.

"Who was our helper?" I asked, squinting up at the trees.

"Not sure. I saw somebody when the first shots came out of there." He lowered his gun. "But they're gone now."

We turned to the fire ring.

The skinhead was dead. The entire right side of his body was soaked in blood, an expression on his face that assured me my bullet had caught him by complete surprise.

I wanted to feel good about that, but I couldn't.

The first thing that had struck me about Malia Moreno when we'd met her at her home was the color of her eyes. They were the same unique amber shade as her brother's, the kind of eyes that stopped you in midstep.

Now, lying in the dirt, the right one still looked like that, still held on to that mesmerizing quality as she stared up at me.

But the left one was gone, taken by the bullet that had taken her life, replaced by a socket full of red, thick blood.

34

I'd called 911 and reported what happened. The local sheriff's department arrived quickly, took our guns, cuffed us, and questioned us about the four dead bodies on the ground.

Carter refused to say a word, staring aimlessly into the forest.

I told them who we were, that we'd followed Lonnie and Mo out here so that we could talk to them and had seen what was happening to Malia. We'd had no choice but to shoot. I told them to call Wellton. They probed further, but I gave them nothing else, preferring to wait on Wellton. They were annoyed by that and kept the handcuffs on us while we sat in the dirt.

Wellton emerged from the pines and walked toward us from the other side of the clearing.

"Oh, look," Carter said. "A forest dwarf."

Wellton was halfway across the circle when he whistled at one of the deputies and motioned for him to head toward us.

They reached us at the same time.

Wellton pointed at us. "Unhook 'em."

The deputy looked uncertain. "Uh, I'm not sure if I'm supposed to do that."

Wellton glared at him. "I didn't ask what you were supposed to do. Do it or you'll be wearing your own set."

The deputy's cheeks reddened, but he produced a key and promptly unlocked both of us. He hurried away, taking the cuffs with him.

Wellton glared at me. "I said you could poke around. I didn't say you could go around killing people."

"Hey, we—" I started, but Wellton kept going.

"You drive out here and just start taking target practice?" he asked, his eyes flaring with anger. "I asked you to help me out. I didn't ask you to drag me into multiple murders. Which part didn't you understand?"

"I understood all of it, Wellton," I said, irritated. "But we had no choice."

"Yeah, you did," Wellton fired back. "You could've put the guns away and called the cops *before* you started blowing people away."

"They were going to rape her," Carter said quietly as he stood up.

We let that hang in the air for a moment and it seemed to temporarily diffuse Wellton's fury.

"Who is she?" he asked.

"Malia Moreno. They brought her here," I said, standing up, dusting off my shorts.

Wellton blinked quickly, chewing his bottom lip.

"Deacon Moreno's sister," I said, answering the question he was trying to put together in his head. "Carter and I met her yesterday."

Wellton turned around and watched the medical examiner's people cover both of the bodies.

He turned back to me, confusion tightening his features. "They killed the sister of a big-time gang leader? How'd she get here?"

"Lonnie and Mo. The two guys that put me in the hospital."

"You saw them bring her here?" Wellton asked.

I recounted how it all went down.

Wellton looked at Carter. "Guns are yours?"

Carter nodded.

"Registered?"

Carter didn't move.

"We'll take them in to confirm ballistics and what Noah's told me," Wellton said, his anger percolating again. "I'll see what I can do about getting them back to you. Maybe."

Carter said nothing.

"There was another shooter," I said.

Wellton didn't understand. "What do you mean, another shooter?"

"Somebody jumped in from where we were watching." I pointed up to the spot. "Whoever it was was with us, though, not against us."

Wellton looked up at the ledge. "They weren't shooting at you?"

"No."

Wellton ran a hand through his short hair. "Either of you get a look at who was up there?"

We both shook our heads.

He exhaled, clearly puzzled. "Alright. We'll check for casings and anything else we can find up there." He turned around and looked at Malia. "Tell me about her."

"Lonnie shot her," I said. "He was the only one near her at the end. I'd already put the other guy down." I explained the rest of the chaotic scene, going back to when we'd arrived up until the sheriff's people got to the scene.

Wellton took a deep breath. "Peter Pluto hires you to find his brother, Linc. You find Lonnie and Mo at Peter Pluto's house. Pluto's dead and they nearly kill you. Then they come after you again." He chewed on his bottom lip again for a moment. "You go looking for Deacon Moreno, talk to him and his little sister, and then she ends up here on the end of a rope pulled by one of the guys that killed your client. Which puts us back where we started."

"It's not Noah's fault," Carter said.

"I don't know why they went after her," I said, thinking Wellton was insinuating the same thing.

"I didn't say you did," Wellton said. "But it seems like your conversations with the Morenos might have triggered this."

I didn't see how or why that was possible, but I could see the trail of his logic. I was positive, though, that we hadn't been followed into either Moreno's neighborhood or to the campground, so I found it hard to believe that this was a reaction to something Lonnie and Mo had witnessed.

"No way all of this is a coincidence, though," Wellton said.

"Not a fucking chance," I said, shaking my head.

"Then how does it all tie together?"

I shook my head again, frustrated at hearing it all laid out in front of me. I couldn't connect the dots. And I didn't know why Malia was brought here, but I knew that it couldn't have just been for random reasons.

The people from the medical examiner's office lifted Malia's covered body and placed her on a gurney. Clouds of dust rose up into the air as they rolled the gurney away and I felt an empty pain in my gut.

"There's one thing that seems to connect all of this," I said, wondering how long the image of Malia's face would haunt my thoughts.

Wellton shoved his hands in his pockets. "What's that?"

"Linc Pluto," I said.

"Who you haven't been able to find," Wellton reminded.

"I'm gonna find him," I said, surprised by the edge in my voice.

"We cleared his apartment, by the way," Wellton added. "Found the weapons and brought them in."

The medical examiner's people came back and picked up the body of the kid I'd shot. The image of him over Malia flashed in my head. I can't say I felt badly that he was dead.

"You find anything else there?" I asked.

Wellton shook his head, but I could tell he was thinking about something else.

"What?" I asked.

"I'm thinking about what happens when Moreno hears about this."

Carter let out a low, long whistle.

"Yeah," Wellton said, acknowledging Carter's whistle. "Moreno's gonna go off." He paused. "And you two could be on his list."

"Why?" I asked.

"Because you were here," Wellton replied. "He'll find out one way or another. And he's gonna hold everybody who was here responsible."

Carter shrugged. "We're on a lot of lists."

Wellton shifted his gaze from Carter to me. "I know. Just watch your asses. I'll do what I can to put it out that you were the good guys here. But a guy like Moreno may not give a shit."

At that moment, I didn't care about Deacon Moreno. He could do whatever he needed to do. I was concerned about only one person.

Linc Pluto.

35

I needed the water.

Carter and I drove back to Mission Beach. He left the second we arrived at my place, saying he needed a nap. I knew that even Carter—tough, indifferent, and rarely bothered—needed to decompress in his own way after our bloody altercation.

I changed into a pair of navy board shorts and a red rash guard, grabbed my board, and headed out.

The beach was nearly empty in the late afternoon, the gray skies probably more responsible than the time of day. The sand felt cool under my feet. The water was greener than it was blue and greeted me with soft ripples at the end of the sand.

Goose bumps rose on my arms as I walked into the chilly water. I slid onto the board and duck-dived under the first two small waves that came at me, the salt water dripping down my forehead, stinging my eyes as I came back up for air.

I paddled out past the break line, but instead of sitting up and watching for the sets, I stayed down on the board, the side of my face resting on the waxy fiberglass, my gaze fixed out over the flat ocean to the west.

The image of Malia's face wouldn't leave me. Carter and I had done what we could, but it hadn't been enough. I could deal with that because we hadn't expected to encounter such an ugly situation. Seeing her life end in such a hideous way was going to leave scars that I didn't think would fade.

Swells formed on the horizon and I sat up. I spun around and got myself into position, paddling just as the water rose beneath me. Popping to my feet, I shifted my weight hard against the wave and sped down to the bottom. I cut back to the top and snapped the nose of the board through the lip of the wave, grunting as I twisted my body with more force than usual. The ocean spray freckled my face. The nose whipped back toward the bottom and bounced on the last breath of the wave as it closed out and dissolved into the ocean.

I went back out several more times, pushing my body harder through the water than it was used to. Anger and frustration fueled my muscles and I wanted my body to feel tired, sore, and empty.

I trudged out of the water an hour later, salt sticking to my arms and face, mission accomplished.

A familiar face slowed me as I came up the sand.

"Started to wonder if you were gonna stay out there all night," Liz said, sitting on the wall that surrounded my patio.

She was the last person I expected to see, but I

wasn't disappointed. I crossed the boardwalk and leaned my board against the wall. "Thought about it."

She wore a black T-shirt, faded jeans. Her hair was pulled back away from her face, mirrored sunglasses resting atop her head. Her blue eyes looked gray beneath the overcast sky. A thick brown folder was next to her.

I sat down on the wall next to her and pushed the wet hair off my forehead. "Needed the exercise."

"It looked like more than exercise to me."

I watched the water, the waves getting smaller as the tide pulled the evening in. "Did it?"

I felt her shrug next to me.

"What do I know?" she said. "I don't surf and you've never offered to teach me."

I looked at her, surprised at her interest. She'd never mentioned it in all the years I'd known her. "Is that a request?"

She met my gaze. "Maybe."

We stared at each other for a moment; then I laughed and looked away.

"John said you had a tough day," she said.

A small spark dissipated inside me as I realized she wasn't just there to say hello. "Wasn't the best."

Purple and orange strands punched through the gray marine layer and tickled the horizon as the sun hit the edge of the water.

I glanced at her. "That why you're here? Wellton wondering if I was okay?"

"John asked me to take a look at some of the paperwork," she said, dodging the question. "I just did some quick nosing around. You knew that the Pluto father was involved in this National Nation crap, right?"

"Yes."

"Did you know that the main suspects in his murder were gang members?"

"No."

"Nobody was charged, but two witnesses gave descriptions that matched a couple of bangers, low-level guys. Turns out they were known associates of Wizard Matellion. They had alibis, but the case notes indicated they were soft. Since Anthony Pluto wasn't an upstanding citizen, no one really gave a shit and the case dead-ended." She pushed the brown folder in my direction. "I didn't have time to read through the whole case file, but I thought you might find that interesting. Keep it for as long as you need it."

Liz had found a solid connection between Linc, the skinheads, and the gang, and that gave me encouragement. There were still some gaps that needed to be filled in, but she had tightened some of the gaping holes and I hoped that reading through the file might allow me to do the same.

"Thanks," I said, placing my hand on the file. "But you didn't answer my question."

She thought about that, her expression indicating that she was measuring her response.

"John thought I'd want to know that you had a rough one," she said finally. "He knew I'd want to know. And I wanted to make sure you were alright."

We sat there silently, watching the water go flat as the strands of sunlight evaporated slowly. I didn't know how to address what she had said. There was meaning in it, meaning that we never seemed to be able to clarify between us. We danced around both our feelings for each other and our differences with each other, finding it easier to argue and dodge and avoid rather than actually deal with those things.

I was tired of the dance.

Liz stood. "Six months. You never called."

I leaned forward, my forearms on my knees, nodding.

"Yeah, I was royally pissed at you," she said. "So I understand why you might have stayed away at first. But you *never* even called me. Never came to see me. We had that fight at the hospital and that was it—you didn't even try to work things out. It was like our relationship didn't even matter to you. What was I supposed to think?"

I stayed quiet.

"Now we're running into each other again and . . . I don't know." She paused. "I hate saying it, but I've missed you. And everything you've said and done in the last few days—the way you reacted to seeing me with Mike, the junior high put-downs—even if it was all stupid and inappropriate and irritating, tells me you feel the same way."

"I do," I said.

"And I want to believe that, Noah," she said. "I do. Except that it seems like I'm the one that's always making the overtures here. And it makes everything feel one-sided."

"Yeah, but six months ago it was one-sided," I said.

"You walked away from me. You made the decision. Not me."

"Because you, once again, did something utterly stupid that nearly got you killed." She paused. "That scared me. And it angered me because you were only thinking of yourself. Not us."

The conversation we were having now was the same one we should've had the day after the argument—and could've if I'd been adult enough to see that then. Liz had thrown her emotions on the table and I hadn't bothered to take a look. Or do the same.

"You caught me off guard with Mike," I said. "I wasn't expecting any of that."

"I know that. And none of it was meant to piss you off. He asked me out. I said yes."

"I know. But it hurt. Seeing you with someone else." I looked at her. "I don't want to see you with any guy but me."

She pointed at me. "*That's* what I'm looking for. Statements like that. Actions that back that up. That's what I need."

I stared at the concrete boardwalk, the sand scattered around my wet footprints. I wanted to remove myself from all this crap and focus on Liz, be where I wanted to be with the person I wanted to be with. Let everything else fall away and make things right.

But a small part of me knew I couldn't leave the past few days behind. Any attempt at a relationship with Liz would be halfhearted until I could put it all behind me. Permanently. And Lonnie and Mo weren't going to go away just because I wanted them to.

I stood, the grains of sand rough between my bare feet and the concrete. Liz had given me an opportunity. She told me what she needed from me and it was up to me to follow through. If I didn't, I had no one to blame but myself.

"Okay. It's on me, then. It'll change." I pointed at the file. "I'm gonna finish this. Soon. And then it's just me and you. I promise."

Her eyes searched my face, maybe attempting to see if there was anything but sincerity in my words.

I knew there was nothing else for her to find.

"Okay," she said. She walked toward me, touching my arm lightly as she went by.

I watched her walk down the boardwalk toward the roller coaster, turn left at the corner, and disappear, leaving me with all the incentive I needed.

After Liz left, I paged through the file she had given me. It confirmed all of what she had told me, but didn't really provide any more new insights. Still, I was energized by the fact that I could fit Linc, the skinheads, and the gang into the same puzzle now and I decided to drive up to Linc's apartment.

My conversation with Liz had made me anxious to see the end of the case, so I could get on with my life. I'd been to Linc's during the day and hadn't learned much of anything and I wondered if the evening would show me something else.

It didn't.

Three hours of sitting and watching gave me no Linc, no gang members, nor any skinheads. As I headed home to bed, that rush of energy I'd gotten from Liz was turning into frustration.

I got up early the next morning, my body feeling refreshed from the tough session the day before in the water and my mind feeling clear from Liz's visit. I was disappointed by the fruitless time I'd spent outside Linc's apartment, but I was determined not to let that slow me down.

I was pondering how to be more fruitful when the phone rang.

"I know where he is," a female voice said after I picked up.

I didn't recognize the voice. "Who is this?"

"It's Dana. I know where he is," she said, rushing her words.

"Linc?"

"Yeah. I'm in Ocean Beach. Can you get here?"

"Tell me where."

I took I-8 to the point where it ended, down past the Sports Arena and south of Quivira Basin. Robb Field, normally packed with soccer players and their families on the weekends, stood eerily empty on a weekday morning as the freeway dumped me onto Sunset Cliffs Boulevard.

Dana's call had surprised me, to say the least. I was skeptical as to what I'd find when I met up with her, but it was better than sitting around and doing nothing. And she had sounded pretty sure of herself on the phone.

I hung a right on Narragansett, then a left on Bacon, taking me into the heart of Ocean Beach.

OB prided itself on being different than the other San Diego beach communities. No beachfront hotels, no chic eateries that hung out over the cliffs, and no signs that they had bowed to the commercialization that had overwhelmed many of the other seaside areas. Locals only. Local eateries, local merchants, and local residents. Nobody got into anybody else's business and as a result, the neighborhood had become an eclectic mix of aging hippies, college students, artists, and folks who viewed society with a skeptical eye.

I turned left at Santa Cruz and spotted Dana's Xterra just past the stop sign. I pulled in behind her and she jumped out and ran to the passenger side of my Jeep.

"I think he's in there," she said, out of breath, pointing up the block and across the street.

It was an old bungalow, the exterior weathered by the proximity to the ocean. A dilapidated wooden deck fronted the house, decorated only with a red sofa that had seen better days. There was no yard to speak of, just clumps of bushes that had taken up residence. The shingled roof was in disrepair, with rotting corners and a sagging middle. Still, the place wasn't much different than the others around it.

Character, I believe the residents called it.

"You think?"

She nodded. "This morning I heard some banging around in his apartment and it woke me up. I got up and looked out the window and I saw him getting into that car." She pointed again and I saw the brown pickup in the driveway. "I waited until he pulled out of the lot and then I followed him."

"Was he alone?"

"Yeah. But he was already out of the car when I pulled up. I didn't want to get too close. But I'm guessing he's inside."

"Any idea whose house this is?"

"No."

It occurred to me that Dana was really eager to play junior detective and I thought I knew why.

"Did you call Carter first?" I asked.

Her face reddened. "Yes. But he didn't answer. Then I called you."

Impressing Carter had become a priority for Dana.

"Stay here," I said, getting out of the Jeep. "I'm going to go up to the house."

"Wait—he had a bag with him," she said.

Wellton told me the apartment had been cleared out. "Guns?"

"I couldn't tell. But why else would he have been back at his apartment?"

I nodded and closed the door.

Walking up the sidewalk, I came to the front edge of the house and moved carefully along the porch. I stepped onto it gingerly, hoping to avoid creaks and rattles. Nothing emanated from the wood, so I continued up, moved next to the screen door, and listened.

Quiet.

I grabbed my gun from my waistband, held it at my side, and knocked on the door.

Nothing.

I tried the screen, but it was locked. Moving down off the porch, I retraced my footsteps to the fence and looked over it. An empty backyard.

I put my gun back in my waistband and hoisted myself over the fence. I fell to the ground and rolled close to the house and pulled my gun out again, creeping low next to the home until I came to the edge, and peered around the corner.

A small patio. An old hibachi barbecue sat on the ground. No tables or chairs.

I moved near the sliding glass door on the back wall of the house. Taking a deep breath, I crouched down, raised my gun, and pivoted so I was looking straight in through the door.

No Linc.

I rose up slowly and tried the slider. It started to move, but then caught. An old lock making it a little loosey-goosey.

I was starting to doubt Dana. Maybe she'd smoked a little too much pot the night before.

I rattled the door some more, seeing if I could shake it loose.

A figure darted out from the hallway on the other side of the door and sprinted for the front of the house.

I spun and ran back the way I'd come, throwing myself over the fence. I came around the corner of the house to see a young man sprinting parallel to the property in the opposite direction, glancing back at me.

Which explained why he never saw Dana step out from the side of the house and clothesline him with a straight right arm.

The guy fell to the ground in a heap.

Dana looked down at him, then at me. "This is Linc."

37

Dana had stunned him and he was a little woozy, so I picked him up off the ground.

"I got bored waiting in the car," she said.

I was annoyed that she had ignored my directions, but it wasn't the time to argue. "We'll discuss it later."

I set Linc on the couch. I sat down in a ripped leather chair across from him and Dana stood next to me.

Linc looked a lot like the photo Peter had given me and, in person, a lot like his older brother—same dark hair and intense eyes—just a little rougher around the edges. Dirty jeans and a black T-shirt hung listlessly on his body.

His eyes cleared and he looked like he had shaken off the blow.

I was so angry with this kid I didn't know where to start.

I glanced at Dana. "You heard him in his apartment this morning?"

She nodded, staring at him. "The walls are thin. The noise woke me up."

"I dropped something," Linc said.

I turned to him. "You can feel free to shut the fuck up until I tell you to talk."

He didn't flinch, just returned my stare as his mouth closed into a tight line.

"Who the hell *are* you?" Linc asked, moving to the edge of the couch.

My right fist clenched and if I'd been closer, I would've punched him.

"I'm the guy that was hired to find your sorry ass," I said. "Both your aunt and your brother asked me to figure out where the hell you've been because for some unbelievable reason, they seemed to give a rat's ass about you. And if you speak again before I ask you a question, I'm going to choke the shit out of you."

"He's an investigator," Dana said.

Linc finally wavered and he slid back into the sofa.

I took a deep breath, summoned up a little composure, and looked at him again. "Let's start with Rachel. What do you know about her?"

He looked at me for a moment, maybe wondering if I was setting him up to say something so I could jump down his throat again.

He chewed on his lip for a moment. "I know she was shot."

"Any idea who did it?"

He hesitated. "I'm not sure. Maybe."

I felt my blood pressure spike. Wouldn't look good

to murder the kid I was hired to find. I tried a different approach to see if I could get a straight answer.

"What do you know about your brother?" I asked.

His expression soured and it was clear he was in the dark. "Peter? What about him?"

"He's dead."

His features drooped and the sour expression morphed into confusion, the first sign that the tough façade had a real weakness. "What are you talking about?"

Part of me felt bad for dropping the news on him. But the other half of me recognized that he was indirectly responsible for Peter's death.

"He hired me to find you," I said. "He was found in a canyon the next day." I paused. "Killed by a couple of other guys looking for you."

He looked away from me, his eyes focused on the floor. His shoulders bunched, the weight of what I'd said taking him out of our conversation for a moment.

Then he lifted his head up.

"You and I need to talk," he said, then nodded at Dana. "Without her."

"Oh, fuck you, Linc," Dana said, irritated.

He didn't look at her. Just at me.

There was something in his eyes that I hadn't expected to see. It was the same desperation I had seen in Peter's face the day he hired me to find Linc.

"Dana, please. Go wait outside," I said.

"Fuck you, too," she said. "I helped you find him."

"Dana, this isn't the time. You've been a huge help, but right now I need you to give us a few minutes, alright?"

She gave an exasperated sigh and threw up her hands like a great stage actress. "Fine. You don't need me? Then I'm outta here. I'll go someplace I'm wanted. You two dickheads have a great time." She spun on her heel and walked out the front door, slamming it behind her.

I looked at Linc, at this kid who I'd been pursuing for what felt like too long, and thought about how ugly the situation had become. I thought about pulling out my gun and putting a bullet in his chest.

But that wouldn't have given me the answers I wanted.

"Talk," I said.

38

"My brother's really dead?" Linc asked.

"Yeah. You want the details?"

He thought about that for a moment, indecision lingering in his eyes before he finally nodded.

I told him about Peter hiring me, then finding the skinheads at his house, and how they'd killed him. I left out the specifics of what they did to me.

Linc leaned back in the sofa, his face heavy with something between sadness and anger. "It all blew up on me. And now I'm totally screwed."

I had a million questions I wanted to ask Linc. But his body language indicated that he seemed on the verge of unloading his story—where he'd been, what he'd been doing—and I didn't want to get in the way. Sometimes, the best way to get answers is to shut up and listen.

"Maybe that's what I deserve." He shifted his eyes toward me. "You know about our parents?"

"I know they're dead."

"My mom died of cancer." He looked out the window. "It sucked."

"I'm sure."

He studied the window for a moment. "I need help. I don't know how to get out of this on my own."

I wasn't willing to commit to anything yet. "Then you better keep talking."

He drummed his fingers on his thigh, his anxiety trying to work itself out. The anger was now removed from his expression, replaced entirely with a look of desolation and dejection.

"My dad died in a fight," he said with a twisted smile. "He was a skinhead. But he hated that term. He liked Aryan Warrior or Caucasian Centrist." He shook his head. "So fucking stupid."

"You don't believe in that stuff?"

He raised an eyebrow. "That's what you've heard, right? That I followed in his footsteps?"

"Yeah."

"You have to be really fucked up to believe in that shit," he said. "I'm not."

I resisted the urge to point out that non-fucked-up college students didn't usually sell guns.

"Then why did your aunt tell me you were involved?" I asked.

He ran a hand through his hair and took a deep breath. "I wanted to know my dad. After my mom died . . . I needed to know him. It was the only way I could figure out how to get close to him." He paused. "I thought if I understood it better, I could find a way to pull him out of it." He paused again. "Peter wanted no part of him. He had just written our dad off, but I couldn't do it. I thought maybe he could still end up being a regular dad. Or at the very least, a dad who was pretty much normal."

Peter had told me about the rift between him and his brother. Peter had probably taken Linc's ideas as lunacy and Linc had obviously taken Peter's resistance as cowardice. Both of them had been half right and all wrong.

"You can't fake it," Linc continued. "To really be accepted, I had to act the part. To everyone, even my family." His eyes shifted away from me again. "And I thought it was the only way for me to really understand what he thought was so great about hating people."

He rubbed his hands together like he was cold.

"But it was . . . awful," he said. "And I didn't understand why my dad believed in it." He leaned forward. "And it just hurt that my dad was such a piece of crap." He looked up, embarrassment and sorrow shaping his face. "Because he really was. Peter was right all along."

I thought about my own parents. I knew next to nothing about my own father, something I had learned to conveniently compartmentalize out of my life. I wasn't close to my mother and I still didn't understand why she couldn't pull herself out from the boozy haze that had become her life.

He was telling me a story I knew pretty well.

"I was trying to figure out how to leave National

Nation when my dad was stabbed outside a bar," he said, his voice cracking. "A couple of black guys gave him what he deserved." He paused and cleared his throat, tears clinging to the corners of his eyes. "Only he was my dad, you know? He was an asshole, but he was still my dad."

I stayed quiet, giving him time to compose himself.

He wiped the tears away. "And then I just got pissed at the world. Peter for not trying to help, my friends for not really understanding. My dad got me involved in some hateful shit, but I didn't tell anyone because I was sick of everyone telling me what an asshole he was. I learned that the hard way. I didn't need to be reminded."

He sat up a little straighter. "My dad used my place to stash and sell guns."

"Why your place?"

"He lived out in Bonita and he was worried that his neighbors would get suspicious if they saw too many people coming and going," he answered. "Anyway, after he died, I wanted to get rid of the guns. All these gang-looking guys were hanging around my apartment. It didn't take much to figure out who they were. I knew Lonnie from the group and he told me what to charge and to give the money to him after they were sold. It wasn't hard to hook up and before long I was dealing with them. What the fuck else was I going to do with a dresser full of guns?"

I thought of a lot of things but said nothing.

"I figured I'd just get rid of them and be done with it," he said. "But Moreno and those guys bought a lot.

When I turned the money over to Lonnie the first time I sold, he freaked because it was so much. So instead of only selling what I had, Lonnie kept giving me more. I didn't know how to say no. That guy scared the shit out of me."

I knew the feeling.

Linc shuffled his feet on the floor and the soles squeaked on the wood.

"Then I got sort of comfortable with it," he said, shaking his head. "I was friendly with the gang guys. Lonnie acted like I was his best friend. It was easy. Easier than telling the truth, anyway."

Linc had jumped into something that had overwhelmed him. He'd forced himself into believing that going along was better than getting out. It may have been easier, but it wasn't better.

"But then it changed," Linc said, his eyes moving away from me. "It all completely changed and I had to get out of it."

"What happened?"

He sat still, his eyes focused on the window. "I knew it was wrong, you know? I really did. I knew I was being a coward, and for a while I thought I could live with that. But then . . . I realized I couldn't."

"How were you planning on getting out of this, Linc?" I asked.

"I was just gonna go down to Mexico or to Arizona and lay low for a while," he said. "I figured I'd sort it out when I got out of San Diego."

"So what changed?" I repeated. "It just hit you that it was wrong?"

His gaze on the window was so intent I wasn't sure if he'd heard me.

"Linc?" I said.

"She changed it," he finally answered, his voice catching.

On my initial visit to his apartment, the girls had explained Rachel's relationship with Linc. He wrote her papers and she slept with him in return. Maybe it had turned into more than that for Linc.

"How did Rachel change things?" I asked.

He moved his eyes back to me, confusion on his face. "Rachel?"

"You said, 'She changed it.' How did Rachel change things?"

He shook his head. "Rachel didn't change anything."

Now I was the confused one. "Then who are we talking about?"

Linc Pluto turned back to the window and the tears reappeared in his eyes. "Malia. Malia changed everything."

39

Malia's name exploded inside of my head.

"Malia Moreno?" I asked, making sure I'd heard him correctly.

"Deacon Moreno's sister," Linc said. "Yeah."

I couldn't come up with another name that would've surprised me more.

"How did you know her?" I asked, trying to gather my thoughts.

"I went to make a drop to Deacon at their house a couple of months ago," he said. "She answered the door, Deacon wasn't there, and we started talking. She was going to State, too. It just sort of fell into place."

A gigantic knot formed in my stomach. I'd already dropped the news about his brother on him. Now I was going to have to do the same about Malia.

"You were dating her?" I said.

His eyes iced over. "We weren't just dating. I was in love with her."

The way he said it made me feel dumb for suggesting any less. "Did Deacon know?"

"We thought we were being careful." His eyes softened as he chewed on his lip for a moment. "But then Malia was pretty sure Deacon had heard her talking on the phone with me. He started asking who her new boyfriend was. She didn't tell him, but I immediately started getting calls from Deacon and Wesley that didn't feel right. They wanted to meet me at different places than normal. I got freaked and that's when I went into hiding." He rubbed his chin. "And then when Rachel was shot, I knew he knew. It was a message to me."

"Have you been here the whole time?" I asked.

He nodded. "Yeah. A guy I know, he's doing a semester abroad. But he kept the lease on the house because he didn't want to lose it. I knew it was empty and I didn't figure anyone else knew about it."

"You said Rachel getting shot was a message to you. How do you know that?"

He sighed and sank back into the couch. "Dana told you about me and Rachel?"

"Yeah."

"It was before I met Malia. I swear to God."

"Okay."

"When I started selling the guns, Deacon and his guys didn't know me. So I had to act friendly with them. Hang out, talk shit, and all that, so that they'd trust me." He shook his head. "Rachel walked out of her apartment one day when we were hanging out in the parking lot and they all went crazy, talking about how hot she was and everything."

It was starting to come together.

"And you told them about having sex with her?" I said.

"It validated me with them," he said, his voice straining. "It was dumb and stupid, but it worked." He paused and I thought he was going to cry again. "And even after Rachel and I were done, I kept telling them that we weren't."

"So Deacon didn't like the idea of you and Malia being together *and* he may have thought you were cheating on her?"

He blinked rapidly, tears clouding his eyes, and he nodded.

It seemed like every time Linc had tried to do something right, he'd made things worse.

He used the heels of his hands to dry his eyes and said, "I was there that day you came to her house."

"What?"

"I was the one behind the door," he explained. "She told you she was studying with a friend. It was me."

My gut had tried to tell me that day something wasn't totally right. His explanation confirmed it.

He started to say something, but it caught in his throat. He swallowed hard, tried to compose himself. "And I was there yesterday, too."

Linc was full of surprises.

I shifted uncomfortably in the chair, remembering the scene. "You were?"

"They made Malia call me and tell me where to meet them." He swallowed hard. "I'd been out there a couple of times before when I was with my dad."

"You were the other shooter," I said.

He nodded, his eyes oozing pain.

"Why did they take Malia?" I asked.

"They knew she and I were together." He hesitated for a moment. "Lonnie saw us together a couple of weeks ago. We were having lunch at the pier in Imperial Beach. We were walking back to the car and I saw him with Mo at the other end of the lot. I tried to duck out of sight and thought maybe I had, because they didn't follow us out of the lot." He shook his head. "But I knew it. I felt him looking at me."

I remembered the look I'd gotten from Lonnie at Peter's house. It was enough to make anyone uncomfortable.

"She was supposed to call me after her first class yesterday. She didn't, and I knew something was wrong. When she finally did call, she was crying and screaming," he said, his voice wavering. "They'd been waiting for her in a parking garage at school. Lonnie got on the phone and told me if I didn't show up, he'd kill her."

I gave him a minute before asking my next question, the one that had been in my head since I'd stepped into Peter Pluto's home.

"What did Lonnie want from you?"

His jaw went rigid. "I owe them money."

"From the gun sales?"

"Yeah."

"Here's a question. Why the hell would you steal their money?" I asked, unable to keep the bewilderment out of my voice. "Both your aunt and your brother told me about your trust fund. Did you blow through it?"

"My trust fund only covers school and what I need to live on," he said, irritated. "And that's it. Tuition goes straight to the registrar and I get a monthly stipend deposited into my checking account. It can only be used for that stuff until I'm twenty-five." He paused. "I didn't take the money for me."

I was skeptical that a kid who had recently lost both parents couldn't pull more out of his trust fund if he needed it. "You couldn't get more money from it after both of your parents passed away?"

He shook his head adamantly. "No. I tried. But there were no exceptions to how the trust was drawn up."

I nodded. "Okay. Who did you steal the money for, then?"

He put his hands over his eyes again, pressing his palms into them, like he was trying to force whatever he was thinking out of his head.

He pulled his hands away and folded his arms across his chest. "You saw Malia's house. Her neighborhood. Her financial aid didn't cover everything. She was out of money for tuition. She wasn't gonna be able to finish her last semester. If I could've used my own money, I would have. But I can't. Couldn't. So I took the money from the last sale I made, gave it to her, and told her it was from my trust. She didn't want to take it, but I finally convinced her."

The money explained why Lonnie and Mo had been looking for him when I'd run into them at Peter's house. They killed Peter as a warning for Linc to pay up. And they'd killed Malia because they wanted to stick it to him, since they still hadn't seen the money. And, probably, simply because she was a black girl dating a white guy.

Linc squeezed his hands together tightly, his fingers turning bright red. I wondered whose imaginary head was between his hands.

"Even if I had the money to bring out there, they were gonna kill us. But I didn't know what else to do. I couldn't figure out how to get her out of there. And then it was too late." He shook his head, the misery clenching his features. "I'm so stupid."

I didn't know where I stood on Linc's stupidity. On one hand, he had attempted to help Malia and escape what he realized had become a situation that had spiraled out of his control. But on the other hand, the one that I wanted to slap him with, he had taken the worst route possible to try and make those things happen.

"Why were you back at the apartment this morning?" I asked.

"I wanted to get the guns I had left," Linc said. "I'd already brought some of them here, but I wanted to get the rest. To get rid of them. I was gonna try and find someone else to sell them to, so I'd have some money to get the hell out of here. But they were gone. So I just grabbed my clothes and bailed."

I was glad I had told Wellton about the guns in Linc's apartment, because I felt confident that Linc would've somehow screwed up getting rid of the guns.

"So now what?" I finally asked. "You said you need

my help. You want to escape? Get away from these guys?"

His head snapped up, anger back on his face. "That's what you got from all this? That I'm just some scared kid who doesn't want to get hurt?"

I said nothing because that was exactly what I thought.

He stood. "I don't wanna hide from them anymore, you asshole. Those fuckin' skinheads killed my brother and they killed Malia. As far as I'm concerned, they killed my father, too. Fuck them and their money."

"What do you want, then?" I asked.

"I want you to help me finish this," Linc Pluto said, his voice full of anger, back to where it was when I'd first sat him on the couch. "Finish them."

40

"I'm not gonna help you kill anyone," I said.

Linc stared hard at me for a moment, as if he couldn't believe what I was saying. Then he shrugged. "Fine."

"Fine?"

"I don't need your help."

I stood. "Yeah, you do."

He sneered. "Oh, right. You've done such a bang-up job so far on all this."

The sympathy that I'd been feeling for the kid for the last few minutes was quickly shifting into anger. "And if your brother had been smart and just left you alone, I wouldn't have been dragged into any of this."

He turned away from me. "Fuck off."

I grabbed his arm and spun him back. "Hey. You think I don't feel bad about what's happened? To your brother and Malia and Rachel? I do. And I wanna get it set straight. But you hunting down a bunch of assholes and killing them does nothing. For anyone."

"Does for me," he said, and lunged at me with his free arm.

His fist glanced off my shoulder. I slid my hand down to his wrist and twisted hard. His face screwed up into a knot of pain and I kicked his legs out from under him. He landed with a thud, the air rushing out of his chest.

"You can't even take me out," I said. "And I'm not even close to being as dangerous as Mo or Deacon or any of those other guys."

The adrenaline surge made my skin tingle. I watched Linc lie on the floor and try to get his breath back. He was wincing, the pain in his back probably surprising him. Landing flat on your spine will do that.

"The best place for you is somewhere safe," I said.

He grunted. "Where's that?"

I ignored the question. "I will take care of this," I said. "I'm better equipped."

"You weren't yesterday. You couldn't save Malia."

I resisted the urge to plant my foot in his ribs. "Neither could you, asshole. However, I will make sure Lonnie and Mo pay for what they did to Peter and Malia. And I will make sure that Deacon and his boys back off."

"I can do it myself," he said, sounding like a four-year-old trying to use a fork for the first time.

"No, you can't," I said.

He pushed himself up into a sitting position, reaching around to rub his back. "Why?"

"Why what?"

"Why do you care?" he asked. "My brother hired you. He's . . . gone. It's none of your business anymore."

Lonnie and Mo had made it my business, but I didn't feel the need to explain that to Linc.

"I promised your aunt," I said, telling him part of the truth. "I told her I'd find you."

"You did that."

"My promises are all-inclusive. Finding you means keeping you safe."

"I can keep myself safe."

"Really? That why you're hiding out here? That why you were hiding behind Malia's door when I showed up?"

His chin dropped and he looked away from me, his jaw locked tight.

I sat down in the chair. "Linc, I'm not trying to embarrass you. But you're in over your head right now. You've told me as much. I'll clean it up. It's what I do."

He picked at his shoelaces, his head still hung. He looked like a puppy that wasn't sure how to grow up.

"They killed my brother and my girlfriend," he said quietly. "I'm not gonna let that go."

"I'm not asking you to. I'm telling you that I will take care of it. It's better that way."

He grunted and then looked up at me, confusion and frustration on his face. "What am I supposed to do in the meantime?"

This was the part I didn't know how to explain to him yet.

"I'm gonna put you someplace where no one can get to you," I said, pulling out my cell phone.

He smirked. "Where? The Arctic Circle?"

I scrolled through the phone book, looking for the number I wanted. "A lot closer than that."

The smirk changed to wariness. "Where?"

"Jail," I said.

"What the fuck?" Linc said, leaping to his feet and knocking the phone out of my hand.

Lunging out of the chair, I caught Linc right in the sternum and shoved him backward. His head popped back when he hit the sofa and cracked against the wall. Before he had a chance to recover, I rolled him over onto his stomach and put my knee into his back. A holding cell was the safest place for him right now, even if he didn't understand that.

"Linc, trust me," I said

"Yeah, Linc. Trust the homeboy," a voice said behind us.

I turned around.

Deacon and Wesley were standing in the doorway, each armed and smiling like they'd won the lottery.

41

Deacon jerked his head at Wesley. "Check the rest of the place."

Wesley dutifully moved out of the room with his TEC-9 and disappeared into the back of the house.

"Bring it out," Deacon said to me, fixing a massive handgun on me. "Slow."

I moved off of Linc and reached around to my waistband, pulling out my Glock.

"Lay it down."

I did.

He looked at Linc. "You been runnin' from me, boy."

Linc rolled over and stared at him, no fear or anger on his face. Just resolution.

"But you knew I'd catch you," Deacon said, smiling at him. "One of my boys was watching your crib this morning, and damn if he don't see some dude look just like you hauling ass outta there." His smile got bigger. "Can't nobody run from me."

"Empty," Wesley said, coming back into the room. "Some guns are back here, though."

They were smart. Deacon stood by the front door and Wesley stood behind us. We were in the middle and cut off from any exit.

"I'm sorry about your sister," I said, looking to buy a little time and try to throw him off track.

Rage bubbled up in his eyes. "Fuck you, you motherfucker. Don't talk about my sister."

"I tried to help her," I said.

"Great fuckin' job."

"He tried to help her," Linc said. "We both did."

Deacon's eyes shot fury in Linc's direction. "You didn't fuckin' help my sister, you white cocksucker. It was your goddamn fault that she ended up like she did."

"I didn't want it that way," Linc said. "I didn't. I just wanted to be with her."

"You are so fucked up, boy," Deacon said. "I mean, so fucked up, okay? You think I was gonna let my sister date a little piece of shit like you? For real?"

Linc stayed quiet.

"She didn't need you screwing her up, man," Deacon continued. "She was gonna do something, alright? Get the fuck out of our ghetto house and do something with her life. But then you went and got all gigolo on her. And now she's dead, motherfucker. Dead like you're gonna be."

Linc stared at the floor. "I loved her."

Deacon took a step toward him, his muscles rigid. "What, motherfucker?"

"I loved her."

Deacon shoved the barrel of the gun against Linc's forehead. "Say it again, motherfucker. Say it again."

"He loved her," I said, trying to draw his attention.

Deacon moved the gun in my direction. "What the fuck you know?"

"They wanted to be together," I said.

Deacon's nostrils flared, his eyes ready to burst out of his head. "She ain't here to love now, boy, is she? She gone and neither of y'all did shit to stop it."

"Not true," I said. "Think what you want. I'm sorry she's dead. But Linc and I tried to prevent it." I paused, weighing my words. "If anyone's responsible, it's you."

Deacon took several slow steps back, looking at me in disbelief. "I know you didn't just say that."

"Those guys just swooped in and took her," I said. "Come on, man. No one was looking out for her. You were sleepin' on the job."

Deacon shook his head, anger flooding his eyes. "No. Fuck you, man. This is your fault."

"And what the hell, Deacon?" I continued, figuring I was already in deep. "You always wanna kill guys that date your sister? Maybe if you hadn't shot his friend and acted like a maniac, Linc wouldn't have had to hide from you and I wouldn't have had to start looking for him." I paused. "If he doesn't have to hide from you, maybe Malia is left out of all this. And she'd be alive."

Deacon's hand clenched tighter on the gun. My words weren't backing him off. He was looking for payback for his sister's murder and he wasn't going to stop until he got it.

"And bottom line," I said, "neither of us pulled the trigger."

He blinked and I thought maybe I'd gotten through to him, maybe hit on the tiny part of reason that was left in his mind.

But then it was gone.

"I don't give a shit about none of that," he said. "All I know is my sister's dead and she was fine until you two motherfuckers showed up in her life."

He had a point.

"Wizard give you the okay on this?" I asked, looking to buy some time. "On taking us out? I mean, I know you can't do anything without his approval."

Moreno walked slowly toward me, the gun aimed at the center of my forehead. He pressed the barrel into my skull.

"Listen up, you cocksucker," he said quietly. "I can do whatever the fuck I want. You understand that?"

"Didn't seem that way to me when I talked to Wizard," I said evenly.

"Wizard don't control me," he said, his voice now rising. "No one does. Wizard's in charge 'cause he likes all the business and shit. Thinks he's some sort of professional dude." He shook his head. "He just like the rest of us, just more of a pussy. That motherfucker doesn't even remember what it's like to put a bullet in anybody no more. Lets us do all his fuckin' work now."

I'd hit a chord. Deacon Moreno was not happy being

an underling. He didn't appreciate having to answer to Matellion.

"So fuck Wizard and fuck you," he said.

He pressed the gun harder into my forehead. I could feel the cold metal digging into my skin.

"How's that feel, homeboy?" he asked, grinning like a madman.

"Great," I said, thinking I'd made a huge mistake by ever talking to Peter Pluto on the beach.

"Then you're gonna love this, motherfucker," he said. "Good night."

I didn't want to die looking at Deacon Moreno's face.

But I didn't think I had any choice.

42

The gunshot shattered the silence.

I flinched.

Deacon Moreno's crazy smile melted from his face. He fell toward me.

I stepped back and let him hit the floor. A dark red spot was mushrooming in the center of his back.

Wesley's TEC-9 was pointed where Deacon had been standing.

"People shouldn't talk shit about Wizard," he said, lowering the gun. "Easy to get dead that way."

I looked at Linc. His arms were wrapped tight around his chest, his eyes wide with shock.

"Uh, thanks," I said to Wesley, my heart thumping hard in my chest. "I think."

"Don't thank me," Wesley said. "Just doing what I'm told."

"Who told you to shoot your partner?"

Wesley turned around. Wizard Matellion stepped

into the room, Big Ollie following close behind. Wizard nodded at Moreno's body. Ollie walked over, lifted him up like he was a pen that had rolled off a table, placed him on his shoulder, and headed toward the back of the house.

"You alright?" Matellion asked.

"Fine," I said.

"Was afraid old Deacon might try something like this," he explained. "That's why I had Wesley prepared. We kinda planned on this, so Wesley was instructed to call me—discreetly, of course—and let us know when and where. He made sure a door was unlocked for us."

I looked at Wesley. He'd found a straw somewhere and was now chewing it furiously.

Linc continued to hug himself.

"Don't get me wrong," Matellion said, grinning. "I'm not in love with you or nothing. I just can't deal with insubordination. Shootin' folks has its place, but not when it's not called for."

The logic of criminals had saved me.

"You asked the other day about a couple of things," Matellion continued. "I did not know about either the girl or the incident that involved you. You made me aware. But those things were done without my permission. They were personal for Deacon and that was unfortunate."

"So he definitely was the person who shot the girl at the apartment?" I asked.

Matellion looked at Wesley.

"Deacon was pissed that his sister was dating a

white dude." Wesley explained. "Then, when he found out this dude wasn't even square with his sister, he went cold crazy." He paused. "He couldn't find this dude, so he decided next best thing to do was to get the other girl."

His use of the word "he" was interesting. I assumed Wesley had been along for the ride for what had occurred but was hanging it all on Deacon. Understandable, now that Deacon couldn't defend himself.

"Then he seen you at the girl's apartment when he rolled up," Wesley said. "Had to wait for you to leave before he could get it done."

"Did he know who I was?"

A wry smile formed on Wesley's face. "Next morning, Deacon sent one of our boys back to the apartment." The smile got a little bigger. "That fat white dude will tell anybody anything for a price."

Rolovich. What a surprise.

"So, when he heard you was an investigator, he thought you might get to this dude before he did and Deacon wouldn't have been able to take care of business. He wanted white boy here all to himself," Wesley continued. "That's why the thing happened with you down in Mission Beach. Was hoping to put you out of commission."

"What do you mean, I wasn't square with Malia?" Linc asked, coming back to life.

Wesley eyed him for a moment. "Man, you told us about the other chick. What Deacon supposed to think?"

"It was bullshit," Linc said.

Wesley shrugged.

Linc dropped his head into his hands. "Nothing happened with Rachel after I met Malia. I wouldn't have done that."

I looked at Wesley. He shrugged again.

"I couldn't care less about any of this," Matellion said, rubbing his chin and looking at me. "I trust that as far as y'all are concerned, nothing happened here today?"

"You give me your word that you have no interest in him?" I said, nodding at Linc.

"I'm gonna forget his name as soon as we walk out of here," Matellion said, grinning and flashing those bright white teeth.

"Then we're gonna forget we were ever here," I said, ready to get the hell out of there.

"One more thing," he said, shoving his hands in the pockets of his sweatpants. "You know who killed Malia Moreno?"

"Why?"

"Deacon may have acted without my permission, but he was still a brother," he said, his voice dropping. "And I look out for my brothers. Any motherfucker that messes with my brother's family messes with me. Know what I'm saying?"

It would have been so easy to pass along Lonnie's name to Wizard Matellion. He could've taken care of him and Mo in any number of ways that wouldn't have involved me. Wiped them off the face of the earth and made the world a better place with no one the wiser.

"No," I said. "I don't know who did it."

Matellion stared at me for a moment, his eyes hard like when he'd warned us about returning to his neighborhood. Finally, they changed and the killer's edge was gone.

"You hear anything," he said, "you let me know."

He turned and left the room.

Wesley looked at me for a moment, the straw bouncing up and down in his mouth.

"You tell Carter I wouldn't mind another shot at him one of these old days," he said.

Wesley chuckled as he followed Matellion out of the room.

I hoped there wouldn't be any more of these old days.

43

Linc and I drove away from the house in silence. There wasn't much for either of us to say and he seemed to have lost the fight I'd seen in him earlier.

I called Wellton, told him I was bringing Linc Pluto in and that I'd explain when we got there. He didn't seem pleased, but I hung up before he could suggest anything else.

When we arrived at the station, Linc got out without protesting. Wellton met us as we came through the doors.

He looked Linc up and down, then turned to me. "This was the kid you couldn't find?"

"Sneaky. Kids are sneaky."

Linc stared at his shoes.

Wellton waved an officer over. He nodded at Linc and the officer moved Linc's hands behind him and cuffed him.

"Can you just put him in holding for now?" I said.

Wellton lifted his chin at the cop and he escorted Linc down the hallway.

I followed Wellton up to his office.

"This is the kid with the guns, right?" Wellton asked, sliding into the chair behind his desk.

"The guns belonged to his father," I said, sitting down in the metal chair opposite the desk, trying to buy Linc a little leeway. "Maybe he didn't know they were there."

"They were where his underwear should've been."

"He's had a rough time of it. He'd be a huge sympathy case if you charged him."

Wellton shook his head. "Fine. Wanna tell me why I'm holding this kid, then?"

I explained about Dana finding the house in OB, my conversation with Linc, and our surprise visitors.

"You're telling me Wizard Matellion saved your ass?" Wellton said when I'd finished.

"Not on the record, I'm not. Off the record, yeah, I guess he did."

"We go on the record, I'd have something solid on Matellion," Wellton said quietly. "Finally."

"Matellion didn't pull the trigger and I'll never repeat what I just told you."

The room went quiet. Wellton couldn't make me talk, but he could make my life difficult. But I wasn't sure he could make it more difficult than Wizard Matellion if I went back on my word.

"Just because he didn't let Moreno kill you doesn't make him a good guy," Wellton said.

"I know that."

Wellton stared hard at me for a while. It didn't change my mind.

"What do you want me to do with this kid?" he finally asked.

"Can you hold him for a little bit?" I asked. "Let me see if I can fix the rest of this."

"What does *fix* mean?"

I shrugged.

"You'll have to be more specific," Wellton said. "I don't understand white-guy nonchalance."

"There are still some loose ends," I said. "He's safer here for a little while."

"What loose ends?"

"Just a few things, couple of people I need to talk to."

We stared at each other, him trying to read me, me attempting to keep him from seeing anything.

"What about our skinhead friends?" Wellton asked.

"That's why I want Linc here. They still want him."

"You gonna go talk to them, too?" he asked, a tiny smile mocking me.

"Something like that."

The smile disintegrated and he pointed a stubby finger at me. "As soon as we—and by we, I mean those of us that are cops—find them, we've got them on assault for you and two murders. That's enough to make me forget about the weapons charge against Pluto. And that's plenty enough reason for them to stay alive."

"If you find them."

"We will find them," he growled.

I sat motionless. I thought back to my first conversation with Professor Famazio, when he indicated that sometimes the skinheads benefited from friends in higher places. Sometimes even the law wasn't enough.

"Neither of them is worth it," Wellton said quietly, his eyes staring intently at me over the desk. "Neither of them."

"I know that."

"I know that you *know* that, Braddock. What I want to make sure of is that you don't do something in spite of it."

The silence sat heavy in the room between us for a few minutes.

"What happened to you sucked," he finally said. "No doubt about it. But if you take them out, if you do exactly what you say you're trying to prevent from happening to the Pluto kid, then you haven't helped anyone and you've completely fucked yourself up."

I didn't disagree with anything Wellton was saying. All of his words made sense. But there were other things that made sense to me, too, and I wasn't sure which of them was more right.

"I'm talking to a brick wall," Wellton said, disgusted at my refusal to engage in the conversation. He shook his head and rolled his eyes. "Shouldn't even try." He paused. "I'll hold the kid for forty-eight hours."

"That's it?" I said.

"That's it," Wellton said. "Do whatever you're gonna do. Make it right." His eyes narrowed. "For Pluto. Not for you."

I was pretty sure he knew his words were going to be in vain. I could see it in his eyes, hear it in his tone.

Or maybe he just knew I didn't care what he said.

44

I drove back to Mission Beach and found Carter and Dana sitting in my living room, a plate of enchiladas on the coffee table as they watched the Padres game.

"We're up five-zip," he said, pointing at the television. "Bottom of the eighth."

"Good."

Dana twisted in my direction. "Where's Linc?"

I nodded at Carter. "You tell him what happened?"

"Yeah, right up to the point where you kicked me out of the house," she said, still annoyed. "I was so pissed, I just got in the car and left. He finally returned my message from this morning and told me to come over here."

"Yeah, well, thanks for that. Because if you'd stuck around you might've been able to warn me that Deacon fuckin' Moreno found Linc, too."

Her eyes widened.

Carter picked up the plate of enchiladas and stuck a fork in one of them. "Tell us."

I told them about all the fun in OB.

"Wesley said that?" Carter said when I was done, placing the now-empty plate on the table. "That he really wanted another shot at me?"

"Yep."

Carter chuckled. "I'll remember that. So now Pluto's in jail?"

"Yeah."

"Why did you take him to jail?" Dana asked. "Won't they arrest him because of the guns?"

"It'll be fine," I said, trusting Wellton.

"As much as I hate anything to do with the law, jail for him is probably the safest place at the moment," Carter said.

"Also keeps him out of the way."

Carter raised an eyebrow. "You make it sound like we're about to do some exciting things."

Dana slid closer to him on the sofa. "Hey. You told me we were going to be the ones doing the exciting things later."

"And I always keep my promises," he said, flashing a grin at her.

"You better."

"Christ," I said. "Keep your clothes on. I'm still here."

Carter looked at me. "Anyway, exciting things."

"Depends on how you define 'exciting.' "

"A Padres victory. Waves that are overhead. Thongs on blonds."

"Then, no. You misinterpreted what I said."

Dana cleared her throat.

"I meant thongs on you," Carter said to her. "Really."

"Thank you," she said, turning back to the TV.

I pointed to the glass slider and Carter nodded.

"We'll be right back," he told her, standing up.

She watched us head for the door. "At some point, I'll start to take this personally."

Carter stood in front of me in the doorway. "I'll make it up to you. In every way."

She smiled. "Fantastic."

I shoved him out the door and closed it behind us.

The ocean air hit me hard and I took a deep breath, letting it fill my lungs.

Carter straddled one of the patio chairs, his arms crossed over the back of it. "Why'd you lie to Matellion when he asked if you knew who killed Malia?"

I wondered if he'd picked up on that. Should've known.

"Didn't see the point of sending him after them," I said.

"Why'd you just lie to me?"

I laughed, but didn't say anything.

"Don't get me wrong," he said. "I'm happy. Means we get to go get them ourselves."

"Figured if we go get them there's a better chance they actually end up in jail," I said.

"If a little worse for the wear."

"You better believe it."

"When do we go find them, then?" he asked.

"Tomorrow, I think." I paused, watching the lines form in the water. "Look, I'm not sure what's gonna happen when we find them. But it's probably gonna get ugly. You cool with that?"

"Cool with that? Are you serious?"

"Just putting it out there."

"Dude, I am down with whatever happens. As far as I'm concerned, with what they did to you, if we're the last ones to ever see them," he said, his eyes narrowing, "good for the rest of the world."

I couldn't have agreed more.

45

Carter and Dana left to go do their exciting things and I tried not to think about it.

I changed into a pair of board shorts and grabbed my board and trudged down to the sand in the hazy, early evening sunshine.

The tension and soreness that had riddled my body for most of the day emptied itself out into the ocean. The waves weren't great—three-footers that were a little mushy—but they were enough to give me what I needed. Lots of little maneuvers that took concentration and forced me to think only about what I was doing in the water. The water was never deceiving. What you see is what you get and I would always appreciate that.

An hour and a half later, I was showered and sitting in front of a sandwich and a Red Trolley when I dialed Wellton's number.

"How's Pluto holding up?" I asked after we exchanged greetings.

"He's fine," Wellton said. "Pissed, but he's fine. You make any progress?"

"Come on," I said. "I just left you a couple of hours ago."

"I'm not kidding, Braddock. Unless you want me to charge him—and I'm still not promising I won't—I can't hold him for more than two days."

"I'll give you a call when I know something," I said.

"I'll hold my breath."

"Don't do that. Guy your size can't have that big of a lung capacity."

"No, but my dick's bigger than anything you've ever seen."

"Let's compare next time," I said, trying not to laugh. "Hey. Is Liz around?"

"She speaking to you?"

"Sort of."

"Probably like that for most people." I could almost hear him smiling. "Hang on."

I'd thought about Liz a lot while I was on the water. It was time for me to do something more than think about her.

"Noah?" she said, her voice filling the line.

"Yeah, it's me. Catching you at a bad time?"

"No. It's fine. What's going on? John said he's got the Pluto kid here."

"Yeah, he does, and he's helping me out by keeping him," I said. "I'll owe him. But he can fill you in on that."

She paused. "Okay."

"You wanna get out of town this weekend?" I said

before I chickened out. "With me? I was thinking of heading up to Santa Barbara. Maybe I could give you those surfing lessons."

My words sounded rushed, awkward, and lame to me as I played them back in my head waiting for her response.

"For how long?" she said finally.

"I was thinking Friday until Monday, but we can go whenever. We could leave Saturday morning or come back Sunday night. If you want to go."

"No, Friday to Monday is good," she said. "Yeah. I'll go."

I'm not sure what I was expecting, but it wasn't a quick agreement. "You sure?"

"Don't make me rethink it, Noah," she said. "You asked and I said yes."

"Right," I said. "I'll pick you up around eight, then, on Friday morning. We'll stop and get breakfast somewhere."

"That sounds nice."

All of it did sound nice. I was glad I'd screwed up the courage to ask her.

"Okay. I'll see you then."

"I'll be ready," she said, and hung up.

It was Monday. Friday seemed a long way off. I needed to get through the rest of the week first.

And then, maybe, I'd finally be ready for Liz.

46

The next afternoon the traffic was light moving out of Mission Beach and back over toward USD. I needed to talk with Professor Famazio again before I made my next move, and I didn't want to do it over the phone. I'd called his office several times in the morning but kept getting his voice mail. I got tired of the phone calls and walked into his office as he was packing up his briefcase.

"Mr. Braddock," he said. "You're still alive."

"Dumb luck."

"The dumb part I believe."

"Do you have a minute?" I asked. "Was hoping you could help me with something."

He looked at his watch. "I've got about ten minutes before our department meeting." He gestured at the chair across the desk. "Sit."

I slid into the chair. "I'll be quick. You mentioned before that you had a database of information. Names, addresses, records. I was wondering if you might be able to check for a name and address in it."

He was leafing through a stack of papers on the desk. "I suppose. Can I ask why?"

"Part of the investigation," I said. "I got a name and I'm trying to track him down."

He looked at me. "Tell me first about the campground. Did you go?"

I told him what had happened. He had, after all, tipped me to the location and what was going on.

"You knew the girl?" he asked.

"Very briefly. I met her while looking for the kid."

He shook his head. "Animals."

"Yeah. Everything you've told me has been dead-on."

"One of the few things I'd rather not be right about." He swiveled in the chair toward a laptop on a small desk to his left. "You have a name?"

"Lonnie."

"Last name?"

"Don't know."

He tapped the keys. "Any distinct body art?"

"Swastika above his eyebrow. His partner had WHITE IS RIGHT tattooed on his forehead."

Famazio chuckled softly. "Superb."

"His name was Mo. No last name on him, either."

He tapped the keys a few more times, staring intently at the screen. He leaned back in the chair. "Lonnie Kerrigan. Several assault convictions. Twenty-six years old with a swastika on his head. Sound like him?"

My heart pounded a little faster. "Yeah."

"It's a Santee address." He scribbled it on a piece of paper. "Other guy's name was Mo?"

"Yes."

Famazio looked back at the screen. "He's also in here. Last name Barnes. Done jail time, too. Same address."

"Not surprised. They seem tight."

He slid the paper across the desk to me. "Should I even bother warning you about these two? What I've got on them indicates that they are two particularly hateful individuals."

"I'm aware of what they are," I said, my voice carrying more edge than I had intended.

Famazio stared at me for a moment. "Yes, I guess you are. No warning, then."

I stood. "Thank you for your help. Again."

His eyes were probing me, searching. Finally, he got up from behind his desk.

"You're welcome," he said. "And I hope it goes well for you."

"It?" I asked, shoving the piece of paper in my pocket.

"Whatever you are planning for these folks," Professor Gerald Famazio said. "I hope it goes well for you."

47

I was driving back to Mission Beach, trying to ignore the weight of the slip of paper in my pocket, when my cell phone rang.

I didn't recognize the incoming number. "Hello?"

"Noah, it's Berk. You in the middle of something?"

"No, I'm just heading home. What's going on?"

The line buzzed for a moment.

"I think I stepped on your toes."

"What do you mean?"

"The thing at Liz's office," he said. "Something was out of place and I think it was me."

I felt my cheeks flush, even though we were on the phone. "Well, I, uh . . . ," I mumbled, not sure what to say and feeling awkward.

"Come on, Noah. It was pretty obvious. I got in the middle of something with you and Liz. I saw it the other night at the bar, too. I didn't know and I'm sorry, man."

"Not your fault," I said. "It's complicated."

"Regardless. That's not my thing," he said. "And I want to apologize."

The truth was, I'd been pissed at him. It was petty and it was dumb, but I couldn't get the picture of him and Liz out of my head. Sometimes I thought like a fifteen-year-old.

I appreciated his apology. "None needed, Mike. Really."

"Good," he said. "Now, I've got the Pluto stuff you wanted."

"Anything good?"

"Well, I'm not exactly sure what you'd think is good at this point," he said. "You got time to come over to my place and take a look?"

"Right now?"

"I'd bring it down to you, but I rolled my ankle playing ball yesterday," he said, sounding embarrassed. "Stupid lawyer's league. Anyway, I'm hobbling. We can have a beer and look at the stuff and you can explain to me these complications with Liz."

"I'm not sure I even know what the complications are," I said, laughing.

"Then we can pretend."

I didn't need the Pluto stuff anymore, but he'd gone through the trouble of pulling it out for me and I was still curious if what Linc had told me about the trust was the truth. I didn't have anywhere else to be and it would give me time to figure out what to do with the address Famazio had given me. "Okay. You still on Mt. Helix?"

"Yep. You remember how to get here?"

"Yeah. I'm in Mission Valley. I'll head up there now."

"Cool," he said. "See you in a little bit."

The phone beeped again as soon as I hung up. Carter's number flashed on the readout.

"Hey," I said.

"What's shakin'?" he asked.

"Going up to Berk's for a beer," I said. "Wanna join us?"

"Where's he at?"

"La Mesa. Mt. Helix."

"Awfully far for a beer."

Carter subscribed to the theory that there was no life east of I-5.

"It's not that bad," I said. "He won't care. Come up."

"Give me the address."

I did.

"Any plans for today that I need to know about?" he asked.

I thought of the address in my pocket. "I'm working on it. You come out to Berk's, we can figure it out."

"I'll think about it," he said. "If I don't show, call me when you're done. Let's get this over with."

I hung up, feeling the same way.

48

Where you live on Mt. Helix dictates your economic worth. The folks at the base of the area were the middle class and the salaries escalated as you worked your way up the mazelike configuration of streets. When Mike had made partner at his firm, he'd moved from his downtown apartment to a ranch house about halfway up the hillside. It had a pool, a game room, and a barely visible view of the ocean if the air was clear enough. He'd worked hard, made a lot of money, and he didn't mind showing it off.

I pulled up in the crescent-shaped drive and stepped out into the late afternoon air. The sun was starting to slide away into the haze.

He greeted me at the front door.

"That was quicker than I expected," he said, extending his hand.

We shook. "The benefits of being my own boss. I don't have to ask for permission to leave the office early."

He laughed and stepped back. "Come on in."

"I invited Carter up," I said, stepping past him. "Hope that was alright."

He hesitated, then shrugged. "Sure. More the merrier."

The cathedral ceilings made the house feel twice as large as its actual three thousand square feet. I followed him down the tiled hallway into an expansive circular living room that housed a pool table and a wet bar.

"Beer's good?" he asked, walking down the couple of steps that led to the sunken bar area backed by a mirrored wall stacked with shelves of expensive liquor.

"Fine. Whatever you got."

Floor-to-ceiling windows showcased the pool and the view to the west. The haze was covering up the ocean and the light was being squeezed out of the day.

Mike pulled two Coronas and a lime out of a small fridge and yanked the tops off the bottles with an opener. He pulled a paring knife from a drawer, split the lime, and stuck a piece in the top of each bottle. He slid one across the bar top to me.

He held his up. "To friends."

"Absolutely."

We clinked the bottle necks and drank.

"Noah," he said, a little uncomfortable. "I meant what I said on the phone. I'm sorry about the thing with Liz."

"You didn't know, man," I said. "Don't be sorry."

"Hey," he said, straightening and putting his hands up in mock surrender. "I didn't know there was something between you guys. If I had, I would never have asked her out."

I took a drink from the beer. "It's fine."

"She called me later after I saw you at her office and politely declined any future offers from me," he said, smiling. "After your reaction, figured it was too much of a coincidence."

"Things have been weird between us," I said, appreciating his willingness to overlook my having been a jerk. "But we're trying to get it straightened out."

"Good for you," he said, raising his bottle.

We each took a drink.

"Why her?" Mike asked.

"Why her what?"

He waved the bottle in the air, a bemused look on his face. "You know. Why are you hooked on her?"

"Liz?" I said, surprised by the question. "Well, I don't know. Why is it ever anyone? Just something there, I guess."

He walked over to the windows. The evening was going black beyond the glass.

"Even with what she is?" he asked.

"Yeah, it's weird with her being a cop and me doing what I do," I said, thinking it was a bit of an odd question. "Not sure it will ever be easy for us, and maybe that'll get in the way. I don't know. But there are always obstacles. Right?"

The room was silent for a moment and I watched his reflection in the window.

He turned around. "No. That's not what I meant, Noah."

"What did you mean?"

He stared at me for a moment, then tipped the bottle to his mouth. He emptied it, walked back to the edge of the bar, and set it down. The clink of the glass on marble echoed throughout the room.

Something clicked in my head and everything slowed down.

"Ankle better?" I asked.

He glanced down at his feet. "What?"

"You told me on the phone you were hobbling," I said. "Seem to be moving pretty good, though."

He looked up. "It's feeling better."

We stared at one another.

"What did you mean?" I asked again.

His mouth twisted into a heartless smile. "What I meant was, why would you choose Liz, when she's a worthless spic whore?"

49

It felt like the air had been sucked out of the room with a giant hose.

Mike laughed. "Oh, wait. Sorry. She's only half spic, right?" He held up his hand. "Don't get me wrong. It's good to get a little variety once in a while. That's what I was looking for. Spending time in bed with a little piece of dark meat isn't all bad. But, Noah, come on. The little senoritas aren't relationship material." He smiled again.

I tried to stop everything from spinning in my head.

"You sent Peter Pluto to me," I said.

"I knew you'd bust your ass to find the kid," he said, nodding. "I knew you would. I didn't intend for you to get the shit kicked out of you, but what can you do?" He held up his hands apologetically.

My conversations with Famazio floated into my mind.

"You're one of the backers," I said. "The anonymous donors that back up this shit."

"You call it shit," he said, amused. "I call it straightening out the world."

The anger was rising up in me like a tidal wave. "Racist assholes are capable of straightening out the world?"

Mike laughed and shook his head. "That is old-school thinking, Noah."

"Old-school? The confederate flag and lynchings are out?"

"So to speak," he said, leaning against the bar. "It's a little more sophisticated now."

"Oh, yeah. Your buddies in National Nation seem completely sophisticated."

"Think what you want," he said. "But what I'm doing is right."

His arrogance was infuriating. Realizing that someone I considered a friend believed in all this shit was like a kick in the face.

"Linc is safe," I said. "And you won't get to him."

"He has our money," Mike said, pointing a finger at me. "And he lied to the organization. That's a problem."

"Your money? Are you like the fuckin' Klan treasurer?"

He folded his arms across his chest. "This is for real, Noah. We are going to change the world."

"Spare me. Drunken powwows at a campground won't do it."

"They're everywhere," he said, his eyes narrowing. "Nigger athletes taking white people's money, in the local government, and overrunning this state's universities." He grinned. "Even wetback cops." He shook his head. "It's gonna stop and National Nation is going to be the leader. I'm proud to fund the cause."

"Let me ask you this, Berk," I said, trying to keep control. "Were you always this fucked up?"

His eyes blazed. "I've awakened to the problems in this society, my friend. If you were smart, you'd do the same." He shook his head in disgust. "Instead of defending that nigger-lovin' kid and sleeping with that half-breed."

I fired my beer bottle at his head. He ducked and it smashed into the wall behind him, showering him with glass and fluid.

Mike stood up and glanced at the wall. "I was afraid it was gonna go like this," he said. "I knew you weren't smart enough to see it my way. I am truly sorry for that, Noah. I really am."

I heard footsteps in the hallway behind me. Felt the adrenaline begin its push into my system, ignited by my anger, and now, fear.

"I believe you are acquainted with my associates," Mike said.

I turned around, knowing who was waiting for me.

Lonnie laughed and put his hands together, cracking his knuckles loudly. Mo stood there with the same blank expression I'd seen before.

" 'Associates' is the wrong word, Mike," I said. "I think you meant 'assholes.' "

Lonnie's smile disappeared and he took a step toward me.

Mo waited for someone to tell him what to do.

Mike said, "I'm sorry it's come to this, bro. I really am."

"Fuck you," I said to him. I looked at Lonnie. "And fuck you, too."

"You're dead, cocksucker," Lonnie said. "Dead."

Up until then, I'd feared Lonnie. But standing in that room with him, knowing this was going to finally end between us, the fear subsided and I realized that I hated Lonnie like I'd never hated anyone else I'd ever met. For killing Malia, for killing Peter, and for nearly killing me. If I was going to die, he was going with me.

I fixed my eyes on him. "Come and get me, asshole."

50

Lonnie and Mo moved toward me.

I stood still.

They spread apart, sealing off the room.

Mike stood at the bar, smiling.

I didn't budge.

They got to within five feet of me.

Small beads of sweat appeared above Lonnie's eyebrows. "This is gonna be fun."

I didn't say anything. My gun was in the Jeep. Hadn't figured on needing it in Mike's house.

Mike came up next to me. "Sorry it's gotta go like this, man. But some things are important."

I took a step toward Mo, away from Mike. I felt Mike follow, probably thinking he could help by staying behind me.

Perfect.

I brought my left elbow up and stepped back, swinging my arm around as hard as I could. Mike's throat collapsed beneath the force of the blow. A horrible gagging noise came from his mouth and he brought his hands up as he fell to the floor. An awful way to die, choking on your own windpipe.

I turned back just in time to see Mo wrap me in a bear hug.

His arms were like giant pythons. He had my arms pinned to my sides and he squeezed. We were nose to nose. His face was so impassive he could've been watching television.

Only he was crushing the life out of me.

"Make it hurt, Mo," Lonnie said from behind him.

I tried to struggle free, but it was useless. The more I flailed, the more he tightened his grip. Mo was making it hurt.

I brought my forehead down on the bridge of his nose. He flinched and shuffled his feet, but didn't release his grip.

I leaned back as far as I could and brought my head down again. This time I caught him flush. I felt bone and cartilage disintegrated against my skull and his arms weakened.

He let out a piercing howl and as I tried to wiggle free, he hurled me over the bar.

I slammed into the racks of booze on the wall. Glass sliced into my shirt and bit into my skin. I hit the floor with a thud, the alcohol and busted bottles raining down on me like a storm. The lacerations in my back immediately started to burn and sting, the pain of hitting the wall radiating down my spine.

"Get him," Lonnie commanded.

Mo grunted and I felt the footsteps coming around the bar. I tried to push myself to my feet, slipping on the now-soaked floor, and went back down to my knees.

Then my hand hit something that I thought my help.

Mo came around the side of the bar. Frankenstein with a destroyed nose, blood splattered on his face like cake batter. A corner of his mouth was curled up. The most emotion I'd ever seen from him.

He reached down for me.

I pushed off the floor and lunged at his midsection. The paring knife in my hand pushed into his gut and he gasped.

I shoved as hard as I could and then brought the knife up awkwardly, feeling the flesh and whatever else was in there rip and tear. He gasped again and stepped back. I let go of the knife, now nearly all the way into his body.

Mo stumbled back, his hands shaking and searching for the knife, staring down at the now-very-visible hole in his stomach.

I charged at him, lowered my shoulder, and drove him back and off his feet. He sailed through Mike's picture-perfect glass wall.

Amid the shattered glass and noise, Mo landed on his back on the pool deck, a huge shard of the window pushing its way up through his chest, as if I'd staked him to the concrete.

I was huffing and puffing, and the adrenaline and pain sending my system in overdrive.

A bansheelike scream came from behind me and I remembered Lonnie.

I pivoted and something sharp and metal flashed in the air. I caught Lonnie's arm before the six-inch blade in his hand got to my neck.

Holding Lonnie's arm and stepping in toward him, I pushed his hand and the knife up higher. I brought my knee up into his crotch with everything I had and he screamed. The strength in his arm dissipated and we toppled to the floor.

Now beneath me, Lonnie was still trying to bring the blade toward me. I had his wrist and drove it into the tiled floor. The bones below his hand gave and the knife clattered onto the floor.

I kept his hand pinned to the floor.

We stared into each other's eyes. He started to relax. He'd lost and he knew it.

And then he smiled.

"You think this is over?" he said, laughing derisively. "You think I haven't done jail before? I'll be out in less than three months and I'll take you and that fuckin' kid down."

Again, Famazio's words came back to me. Lonnie knew someone, somewhere in the legal system, would have the power to take care of him.

Lonnie grinned at me. "Just like I did that nigger bitch yesterday."

I moved my free hand to his throat and pressed down. His eyes bulged as his pupils dilated, my leverage winning out as I compressed everything in his neck. He slapped at my hands.

Footsteps echoed in the room. They stopped just before reaching us.

"Noah?" Carter said. His voice sounded like it was in a tunnel.

I eased up on Lonnie's throat, but didn't look at Carter.

Lonnie started to smile again, maybe thinking that it was over now. Probably thinking about how stupid I was for sending him to jail so he'd have another chance at me and at Linc. Almost certainly thinking he would eventually win.

I pressed down again, harder than before, feeling Lonnie's windpipe and larynx pulsate against the palm of my hand.

His eyes bulged more and he started to gag. He started kicking beneath me, slapping again. I guess he realized he wasn't going back to jail, that even his powerful friends couldn't help him out now, and that his chances at me and Linc were over.

Lonnie's kicking stopped. The pulsating in his throat stopped. And finally, the hate in his eyes stopped.

51

Carter and I were standing in the driveway when Wellton walked out of Mike Berkley's house.

Wellton looked at me. "You alright?"

I shrugged. "I'm fine."

"Tell it to me again," Wellton said.

"I came up here because Berkley called me and said he had some things to tell me about Peter and Linc Pluto," I said. "It was a setup. Carter got here at the very end."

Wellton stared at me, his eyes frozen with intensity.

"I took Mike first," I continued. "Mo was next. Lonnie and I were struggling with the knife he brought at me. He wouldn't drop it. I had no choice."

Wellton looked me up and down. "He cut you?"

"I'm cut everywhere. Probably."

Two EMTs rolled a gurney out of the house, a sheet covering whoever's body was underneath.

Wellton caught my eyes again. "So you held off the knife with one hand and choked him with the other?"

I held his gaze. "He wouldn't drop the knife. I had no choice." I motioned in Carter's direction. "Carter will tell you the same thing."

"I'll bet he will," he said.

"Famazio might be able to link Berkley and National Nation," I said. "I don't know."

Wellton remained silent. He didn't move. Just stared right through me.

I didn't care.

"I could give a shit that they're dead," he finally said. "Just taking up my air while they were alive, as far as I'm concerned. So fuck 'em." He paused, chewing on his lip for a moment. "And I'll write it up just like you said. You had no choice. Because I got nothing else."

"I had no choice," I said.

Wellton shoved his hands in his pockets. "But maybe someday you can explain to me exactly what that means to you."

He turned and walked back into the house.

Carter followed me back to my place. I got out of my car and walked over to his monstrosity of an automobile. He cut the engine, but didn't get out.

"We good?" he asked.

"Think so," I said. "There'll probably be some follow-up. But we're good."

Carter nodded. "You okay?"

"Fine."

He stared at me. "Sure about that?"

"Positive."

"I thought about taking you off him," he said.

"I figured."

"Wasn't sure I could, though. You looked different."

"I could've taken myself off if I'd wanted," I said.

"I know. You want my opinion?"

"Always."

"You made the right choice," he said.

I shrugged.

He turned the key in the ignition and the engine rumbled to life.

"I mean it, Noah," he said, leaning across the passenger seat so I could hear him. "It was the right thing and it always will be. He doesn't die today, he would've come after you and the kid again someday."

I didn't say or do anything. I didn't know how to respond.

He held up a hand, dropped the gearshift, and sped away down the alley.

I walked into my place and didn't bother to turn on a light. I went to the fridge and pulled out a beer. Popped the top on the bottle. Set the bottle on the counter. Turned to the sink and vomited.

After a few minutes, I picked up the beer and walked out to the patio. The white foam of the collapsing waves was bright against the black sky and dark water. The wind blew softly off the water and up the sand, whispering against my face.

I didn't regret killing Lonnie, but that didn't mean it would ever feel right. No matter what Carter said or how I justified it, I had taken a life. I would always feel his skin on my hands and see his eyes as they ran out of life. Lonnie hadn't added anything to the world, but I had taken something from it and I wasn't sure how to get back on the right side of the line I'd crossed.

I stood there, watching the ocean and thinking about those things, for a long time.

53

"You mind if we make a quick stop?" I asked.

It was Friday morning and Liz and I had just started north on I-5 for Santa Barbara. I'd tried to reach Linc after Wellton released him from custody, but he hadn't returned my calls and if he'd gone back to his apartment, he hadn't answered the door when I'd knocked.

I called Marie Pluto and told her that her nephew was okay but I wasn't sure where he was. She told me that he'd already called her and was going to stay with her for a while. She thanked me for my time, told me the remainder of my fee would be in the mail the following day, and promised to keep in touch.

I hoped that she wouldn't, but didn't tell her that.

"Sure," Liz answered. "What for?"

I slowed at the off-ramp. "Just want to check on Carolina. I told her I'd call her after we had dinner the other night and haven't had a chance."

"Sure," she repeated, a soft smile on her face.

The thick early morning fog was melting away, leaving a wet haze behind. I figured by the time we got to Santa Barbara, there'd be nothing but sunshine.

I needed it.

We pulled up at the curb and I cut the engine. "You mind waiting?"

"Take as long as you need," Liz said.

I walked up the path to the house, free of the anxiety and questions that had wracked me the last couple of times I'd been to the house. Our dinner had been good and helped cleanse a few things.

Maybe the fractures in our relationship could heal.

I rang the doorbell.

No answer.

I knocked and got the same response.

I turned the doorknob and it opened, so I stepped in.

And right back to my childhood.

There were at least six empty vodka bottles scattered around the coffee table. The stale smell of booze clung to the air and seemed almost tangible. Paper plates and glasses, several days old, were strewn across the carpeting.

Peeking into the kitchen, I saw the sink and counter were full of dishes that hadn't seen cleaning in a while.

I took a deep breath and walked back to the bedroom.

Carolina was passed out on the bed, snarled among the sheets and blankets. Her blouse was wrinkled and unbuttoned. Her makeup was smudged, the mascara having run down past her eyes, giving her face a macabre appearance.

I walked closer to the bed.

Her chest rose and fell evenly, as she breathed out through her mouth.

I'd stood in the exact same spot and seen the exact same thing so many times before.

The relationships that had been destroyed in the last week flashed through my mind.

I had hoped that Carolina and I were repairing ours. But she'd made a promise that she couldn't keep. It wasn't so much about anger as it was disappointment. A week earlier, maybe I would have stormed out of the house and made some sort of declaration about a future without her.

Instead, I pulled the blankets over her as best I could and locked the front door to the house behind me when I left.

I looked at Liz sitting in my car. Her head was back—she was probably dozing. There was nothing I could do about Carolina at the moment. But another chance with Liz was in front of me and that was more than enough to satisfy me for the time being.

I got in the car, stuck the key in the ignition, did a U-turn, and pointed us back toward the freeway.

Her eyes focused on me for a few minutes before she spoke.

As we glided down the on-ramp, she asked, "Everything okay?"

I moved the Jeep into the fast lane, thinking again of Linc, Peter, Malia, Deacon, Lonnie, and my mother. Chances missed and chances taken.

I reached over and covered Liz's hand with mine, determined to find that sunshine up the coast.

Acknowledgments

Once again, it takes a huge cast to make me look anywhere close to good. . . .

Mario Acevedo, Margie Lawson, Tom Lawson, Sandy Meckstroth, Jeanne Stein, Kevin Tracy, and Sue Viders all read some early version of this novel and offered suggestions that made it much better.

My agent Victoria Sanders continues to be an enthusiastic supporter and guiding force—I can't thank her enough, but I'll continue to try.

Big thanks to all the people at Dutton, NAL, and Penguin Group USA who have gone above and beyond to help me, including Brian Tart, Lisa Johnson, Beth Parker, and Molly Boyle. Special thanks to my editor extraordinaire Martha Bushko, who, with much humor, patience, and an unerring eye, reminds me of where I'm trying to go no matter how much I try to veer off course.

To the family and friends too numerous to name—your support the first time around made the whole trip more enjoyable than I could've imagined. Thank you.

To Stephanie and Hannah—I am a grumpy old troll to live with when writing a book. Thank you for supporting grumpy old trolls. I love you both.

Jeff Shelby

Killer Swell

A Noah Braddock Mystery

Noah remembers Marilyn Crier as the stuck-up mother of his high school girlfriend, Kate. Back then she thought Noah was strictly out of her daughter's league. Now she's appeared out of the blue because Kate's missing, and she thinks Noah might be able to find her—for old time's sake. But, as the investigation deepens, Noah discovers more about Kate than he ever wanted to. A lifetime away from high school, she's been traveling in some very dark circles, and Noah is going to have to make some pretty sharp moves if he wants to make it back alive.